He sat there waiting for someone to serve him a glass of rum.

On the other side of the room the free-for-all was gaining momentum. It had passed the phase of rum-induced fury; now it was blood-induced. The more blood they spilled, the more they wanted to spill.

"Come on, I'm thirsty," Bevan complained. He hit his clenched hands against the wooden surface of the bar. "What's the matter here? The bartenders on strike?"

He managed to get to his feet, worked his way slowly and staggeringly across the room, moving through the chaos of all-out combat that enveloped him. He was dimly aware that something hectic was happening, but it didn't mean anything to his liquor-soaked brain.

He had to get that drink, and the need for it throbbed in his brain as he gazed around, searching for the nearest exit. He saw the side door at the far end of the bar and started pushing his way toward it, slowly forcing a path through the swarming, seething mass of wild-eyed men. Somehow they had him listed as a neutral, and without giving any thought to it they refrained from banging at him as he made his way toward the side door.

But there was one Jamaican whose attention had been drawn to the displayed wallet and the thick sheaf of green bills it contained. He detached himself from the whirlpool of battle and his expression was catlike as he followed the drunken tourist toward the exit that led to a dark alley...

The WOUNDED
and the SLAIN

by David Goodis

A HARD CASE CRIME NOVEL

A HARD CASE CRIME BOOK

(HCC-031)

First Hard Case Crime edition: May 2007

Published by

Titan Books

A division of Titan Publishing Group Ltd

144 Southwark Street

London

SE1 0UP

in collaboration with Winterfall LLC

ISBN 978-0-85768-375-5

Cover design by Cooley Design Lab
Design direction by Max Phillips
www.maxphillips.net

Typeset by Swordsmith Productions

The name "Hard Case Crime" and the Hard Case Crime logo are trademarks of Winterfall LLC. Hard Case Crime books are selected and edited by Charles Ardai.

Printed in the United States of America

Visit us on the web at www.HardCaseCrime.com

THE WOUNDED AND THE SLAIN

Chapter One

At the other end of the bar it was crowded, and at this end he stood alone, drinking a gin-and-tonic. They made a very good gin-and-tonic at the Laurel Rock, but he wasn't getting any taste out of it. As a matter of fact, he thought, you're not getting any taste out of anything. And then, as some of us do at one time or another, he played with the idea of doing away with himself.

You could do it tonight, he thought. This is as good a night as any. There's some deep water not far from here, the lukewarm water of the Caribbean. All it needs is something heavy tied onto your ankle. But they claim that's an awkward way to go out, all that choking and gagging and getting all flooded inside, that's a messy business. Maybe a razor blade is better. You sit in the bathtub and close your eyes so you won't see it pouring from your wrist, and after a while you just go to sleep. That would be fine, he told himself. You're certainly due for some sleep. You haven't had any decent sleep for God knows how long.

He finished the gin-and-tonic and ordered another. At the other end of the bar they were having a good time, talking pleasantly with some energetic laughter thrown in. He tried to hate them because they were enjoying themselves. He collected some hate, aimed it, and tossed it, then knew right away it was just a boomerang. There was no one to hate but himself.

And maybe her, he thought. Sure, let's include her. But that wouldn't be gallant, and you've always tried so hard to be gallant. That's one of your troubles, mister. When it needs trying, it's no good. This thing they call gallantry should come easy, come natural. But I guess we're not in that category, he mused. I guess we're designed for strictly off-the-beam operations, like not being able to sleep, not being able to eat, not being able to do anything except think of what a lousy life it is and how you wish you were out of it.

All right, he told himself firmly, let's do it and get it over with.

He took a step away from the bar, took another step and stopped and shut his eyes tightly. A shudder ran across his shoulder blades and down his arms. He opened his eyes and saw the barman looking at him inquiringly.

"Are you all right, sir?" the barman asked quietly and courteously.

He frowned at the dark-skinned West Indian who wore a Piccadilly collar and white tie and spotless white barman's jacket.

"Sure I'm all right." He said it thickly and somewhat rudely. "What makes you think I'm not all right?"

"I thought you might be ill, sir. For a moment there you seemed—"

"Now look," he said to the barman, leaning forward with his hands gripping the edge of the bar, "I'm not intoxicated, if that's what you're implying."

"That isn't what I meant, sir. All I meant was—"

"I don't care what you meant. You're here to sell drinks, aren't you?"

"Well, yes, sir. But—"

"Then sell them. Go tend to your customers and leave me alone."

"Yes, sir." The barman nodded. "Very good, sir."

"And another thing," he said to the barman. "I don't get this 'sir' routine. What is this? The goddamn British Navy?"

The barman didn't answer. He stood there behind the bar, standing erect and dignified and looking very Afro-British with the Piccadilly collar very white against the darkness of his skin. He was proud of his loyalty to the crown, his status as a citizen of Jamaica, and his job here at the Laurel Rock Hotel in Kingston. His face was expressionless as he waited for the American tourist to make another remark about the British Navy.

"I don't like to be called sir," the American said. "It gets on my nerves to be called sir."

The West Indian's face remained expressionless. "What would you prefer to have me call you?"

The American pondered for a moment. "Jerk," he said.

"I don't understand that word," the West Indian said quietly.

"You would if you knew me." He gazed past the dark-skinned barman, absently reached for the tall glass, lifted it to his mouth, and finished the remainder of the gin-and-tonic. He handed the empty glass to the barman and mumbled, "Fill it up again."

"Are you quite sure you want another?"

"Hell, no." The American tourist went on gazing at nothing. "It's the last thing in this world I want. But the point is, it's the first thing I require."

The barman moved away. The American tourist leaned heavily on the bar. He lowered his head to his folded arms and said to himself, You jerk, you. Oh, you poor jerk.

His name was James Bevan and he was thirty-seven years old. He had an average build, five-nine and one-fifty, and average-American looks, straight-combed straw-colored hair, gray eyes, medium-length nose, and his complexion was somewhere between country-club tan and business-office yellow. He wore a custom-fitted dark-brown mohair suit made by a Manhattan tailor whose price was never higher than ninety-five dollars, his shirt and tie were from a Fifth Avenue haberdashery that specialized in good quality at fairly reasonable prices, and his shoes were good but not exceptional dark-brown suede. The clothes more or less represented his weekly income and the type of work he did. He was a customer's man for a Wall Street investment house and he averaged around $275 a week. Usually he was able to save a little of it, but during the past seven months he'd been doing a lot of drinking and buying drinks for strangers and it added up to excessive spending.

Also, during the past seven months he'd been seeing a neurologist about his inability to sleep and his lack of appetite and of course the drinking. In Manhattan there are a great many neurologists and some of them are rather expensive. This nerve specialist that Bevan had been seeing was definitely expensive, and going there several nights a week had caused a severe strain on Bevan's bank account. The neurologist had finally admitted they weren't getting anywhere, and suggested that Bevan should try some other therapy, like, say, a trip somewhere, a change of atmosphere. Bevan had gone home and told his wife about it, and a few days later he talked to his employer and requested a four-week leave of absence. The employer was more than willing to grant it; he liked Bevan and he'd been worried about Bevan's condition. He patted Bevan on the shoulder and told him to play a lot of golf and come back with a nice suntan.

Bevan consulted with a travel agency and they recommended the West Indies, specifically the island of Jamaica. He said that would probably be all right, and they went ahead and obtained seats for him and his wife on a Pan-American DC-6. They also handled the hotel reservations, putting in a call to the Laurel Rock in the city of Kingston.

The Laurel Rock is quietly elegant and traditional and it has an excellent reputation for food and service and management. It is a fairly large hotel, and the grounds surrounding the yellow-brown building are well kept and include a fine garden and a swimming pool. Altogether the Laurel Rock is a place of refinement and distinctive charm, and it is very popular among American and British tourists visiting Jamaica. The hotel is located on Harbour Street and on one side it faces the water of the Caribbean. On the other three sides the Laurel Rock has a fence that shuts it off from the neighboring dwellings. The neighboring dwellings are rather low in real-estate value. It is only a short walk from the Laurel Rock to the slums of Kingston, and these are among the dirtiest and roughest slums to be found anywhere in the Western Hemisphere. Guests at the Laurel Rock are generally advised not to venture beyond the grounds after dark.

Since their arrival at the hotel, three days ago, Bevan and his wife hadn't seen much of Kingston. He was in the bar most of the time, and she stayed in their room, reading or listening to the radio. On their second day he'd asked her if she wanted to go sight-seeing, and she said no. Then this afternoon he'd asked her again and she said no, she didn't feel like going out. He said it didn't make sense to stay in the room and they ought to get some sun out at the swimming pool. She said no and he coaxed her and finally she put her hands to her face and groaned, "Oh, leave me alone. Get out of here and leave me alone." He went out of the room and downstairs to the bar.

She hadn't appeared for dinner and he'd juggled the idea of going up to the room and having another talk with her. But talking with her had become an ordeal, and although he wished desperately they could get on the same track and reach some sort of understanding, he sensed it was impossible, he wasn't up to it. At dinner he'd sat alone at the table and barely nibbled at the juicy rare roast beef that begged to be eaten with gusto. Most of it was left on his plate when he got up from the table and headed back to the bar.

Now it was getting on toward midnight and he had no idea how many gin-and-tonics he'd consumed. But whatever the amount, it wasn't enough. He lifted his head from his folded arms and saw the barman coming toward him with the tall glass three-quarters filled, the bubbles of effervescence dancing around the cubes of ice.

He reached for the glass and was bringing it toward his mouth when he saw her entering the cocktail lounge. She moved toward him like a thin blade of blue-white steel coming in to cut him in half. Here she comes, he thought, gazing dismally at the advancing figure of his wife, and he closed his eyes, wishing he could keep them closed for a long, long time. He was saying to himself, Point One: You can't stand the sight of her. Point Two: You can't stand the idea of losing her. Point Three: What in God's name is the matter with you?

Then his eyes were open, and as she came up to the bar to stand beside him, he said, "Have a drink?"

"No, thank you."

"Hungry? I can order you a sandwich."

"No," she said. "But I'd like a cigarette."

He took a pack of cigarettes from his pocket. "Come on," he said. "Let me buy you a drink."

She didn't answer. He lit her cigarette, lit one for himself. Then he waited for her to say something. Without sound he was begging her to say something, say anything that would establish some line of communication. But all she did was stand there showing him her profile as she took slow, calm drags at the cigarette.

Oh, well, he thought, and shrugged inside himself. But the shrug didn't work, and he snatched almost frantically at the gin-and-tonic. He took several gulps and the alcohol charged his brain with a series of stimulating stabs that brought a dim, half-pleased smile to his lips. The smile became dimmer and somewhat sardonic as he stepped back to give her an appraising look.

This is better, he told himself. This is a lot better than trying to talk to her. He went on giving her the up-and-down look, as though it weren't his wife standing there, but some interesting-looking female he was seeing for the first time.

Really interesting, he estimated. The breeding shows, and you know right away it was first a governess and then finishing school in New England, followed by Bryn Mawr or Vassar, someplace like that. They wouldn't let her attend a coed institution; you can bet they stood firm on that issue.

It was gaining momentum in his brain, and he went on: Stands to reason she comes from people with a comfortable amount of cash. Not exactly in the ultra-ultra bracket, but comfortable enough to own property with considerable ground around it, a two- or three-car garage, maybe some horses, a summer home out on Long Island. Oh, they have it, all right. But check that just-right tilt of her chin, and you know they never lavished the cash on her. She doesn't look the least bit pampered or spoiled. She looks as if she's been guided and guarded very carefully. So the governess must have been Swedish; they're usually the strictest. Then later, when she started going out with boys, there was always a chaperone.

Oh, yes, there had to be a chaperone. And that made it tough on the boys. That is, if they went for the fragile type, the dainty and delicate little lady with the pale-gold hair and pale-blue eyes and very-pale-ivory complexion. You go for that? Yes, I guess you go for that.

The way a moth goes for the blue-white flame, but it turns out to be an icicle that freezes him to nothingness very quickly.

With frozen eyes he stared at his wife and saw the pale-gold hair parted in the middle and sleeked down to partially cover her delicate ears. And the pale-blue eyes, the very-pale-ivory complexion that harmonized with her fragile slenderness. Just a tiny suggestion of bosom and hardly any hips at all. But it wasn't entirely a string-bean build; there was just enough subtle molding of breast and thigh to make it interesting.

Let's get away from that, he thought. Let's get it more in terms of statistics. She's five feet four inches tall. She weighs exactly 109 pounds. She's twenty-nine years old and you've been married to her for nine years. Hey, now, a lot of nines coming up here. Maybe nine is your lucky number. You mean your unlucky number. For instance, it takes nine months to produce a baby, and she hasn't been able to produce one yet. I think you better pull away from number nine. Let's try

a number we all know is lucky, like seven. That's a
good number. Oh, sure, that's a very good number. It's
been seven months since you've done it with her.
That's unbelievable. Yet it's a fact, mister, an irrevocable fact.

And please, whatever you do, don't blame the individual that invented twin beds. The twin beds have
nothing to do with this problem. This problem is
founded on the premise that she doesn't want it and
even if she wanted it you wouldn't be capable. We
might as well put it plainly and say she's frigid and
you've become impotent because of it.

Well, sir, that balances the equation, it makes the
score zero-zero. So what say we have a drink on that?

But the glass was empty. He called to the barman
and ordered another. He heard Cora saying, "I wish
you wouldn't."

He leaned low over the bar, aiming a grin at empty
air. "It's just a way to pass the time."

"Please don't drink any more tonight."

"It isn't drinking, really. It's just taking medicine."

"James, don't talk foolishly. All that gin in you, it
doesn't do you any good."

He was still grinning, still aiming his eyes at nothing.
"I wish there were a substitute."

"I don't know what you mean."

"Don't you? The hell you don't."

The barman arrived with the gin-and-tonic and
placed it in front of Bevan. He reached for it, then
decided to let it stay there for a while. He grinned at
the glass, at the glimmering ice cubes in the bubbling

colorless liquid. He heard Cora saying, "You're getting drunk, James. I can always tell when you're getting drunk."

"Hello," he said to the glass. "Hello, palsy-walsy."

She put her hand on his arm. "Listen to me."

"You really my pal?" he asked the glass. "You wanna be my pal, you gotta stick with me. O.K.?"

"James—"

"It's gotta be true-blue all the way," he said to the glass. "None of this fair-weather-friend routine. What I need is a real pal, someone I can talk to. That's been my trouble, I got nobody to talk to. So let's have an understanding, pal. There's nothing in this world like understanding."

She was pulling at his sleeve. "Will you please listen to me?"

"Can'tcha see I'm busy? I'm busy here, I'm talking to my pal."

"I can't stand it when you're drunk."

"And I can't stand it when I'm not drunk."

He was leaning very low over the bar. She gripped his middle and tried to straighten him. He pulled away from her and stumbled sideways and she said, "James, there are other people in this room. They're looking at you."

"Me?" He was gripping the edge of the bar to keep himself from falling to the floor. "Why they wanna look at me? I'm nobody."

"I wish you'd stop trying to prove it."

"Don't hafta prove it. Got the evidence right here." He pointed to himself. "All wrapped and sealed and labeled fourth-class mail. Better handle it gently, boys, it might fall apart."

Then he reached for the glass and missed and his groping hand went sliding across the bar, his head going down and his chin hitting the polished hardwood surface. He let his head stay there, and heard her saying, "Get up, James. Stand up straight."

"I been trying that for years. Can't do it. Not up to it at all."

"Here, let me help you." She took hold of his shoulders.

He pushed her away. "Don't need any help. Need another drink, that's what."

There was some awkward stifled laughter at the other end of the bar. Cora made another attempt to pull him upright and again he pushed her away. She closed her eyes for a moment, and then said very quietly, "The very least you could do is think of me."

"My dear adorable girl, I'm always thinking of you." And then laughing, biting on it and sobbing it, "Can't ever stop thinking of you."

He tried to straighten himself, but as he lifted his head his knees gave way. Cora grabbed him and he fell against her, his weight throwing her off balance. As they went stumbling away from the bar, a man detached himself from the group at the other end and came hurrying toward them. The man caught Bevan under his armpits, held him upright, then took him to the tables near the bar and put him in a chair. Bevan's head flopped onto his folded arms. He heard a dull humming in his brain, then heard Cora say, "Thank you," to the man. The man said, "Quite all right," and then Cora said, "I'm terribly ashamed." The humming came in again, but through it he heard the man say, "I guess he had too much."

Bevan raised his head and looked at the man. "Now, how in hell did you figure that out?"

The man gave him a tolerant and somewhat amused smile. Bevan decided it wasn't a smile, it was more on the order of a leer. But of course he couldn't be sure about that because now the man was twins and then triplets seen through a wall of glue-stained celluloid. The wall moved in, then tilted abruptly, and he was on top of it and sliding down. He told himself he wasn't ready to go out yet. Inside himself he punched back at the gin that was punching away at his brain. It helped some, and he managed to sit up fairly straight. Again he was focusing on the man. He saw that the man was of average height but on the heavy side, with reddish complexion and carrot-colored close-curled hair. The man had gray-green eyes and his nose was slightly flattened. He wore a beige suit of thick Italian silk and butter-colored buckskin shoes. He looked to be a fairly prosperous and maybe important alumnus of whatever college he'd attended, probably an Ivy League school.

"So who cares?" Bevan mumbled to no one in particular. "I'm a Yale man myself."

The man was looking at Cora. "I'd better take him to his room."

"I hate to trouble you," she said.

"It won't be any trouble."

"Don't bet on that, brother," Bevan said. He smiled amiably at the man and the man smiled back.

Cora said, "We're in Three-o-seven."

The carrot-colored hair and flattened nose came slowly toward Bevan and he widened his smile and said, "You really think you can do it?"

"We'll both do it," the man said. He sounded like a kindly scoutmaster. "We'll make it together, sonny."

"Sonny," Bevan said. "Don't gimme that sonny business."

"Come on," the man murmured gently, moving in close and reaching for him. "Let's give it the old college try. Let's score one for Old Eli."

"Oh, get away," Bevan said wearily. "Get the hell away from me."

"Easy, now," the man said, taking hold of Bevan's arms, lifting him from the chair. "Let's do this nice and easy as we can."

Bevan allowed himself to be pulled upright and when he was sure he had the floor under his feet he pivoted in the man's grasp, yanking himself free. Then he hauled off with his right hand and aimed a roundhouse delivery that went very wide, the impetus carrying him past the man, sending him into a table that overturned. He landed hard on his face, his head resting on the slant of the overturned table. The table drifted away from under him and he was asleep.

They're laughing, Cora said to herself. You can hear them laughing. It isn't the loud raucous jeering laughter, it's more on the quiet tactful side and they're trying to hold it back. But they can't hold it back, it's really such a funny sight. Yes, it's so funny. It's a kind of slapstick, I guess. Can you see it that way? You wish you could see it that way.

She stood there listening to the muffled laughter from the other end of the bar. They were looking at the drunk who was sleeping with his head resting against the overturned table. The heavily built man moved toward the drunk and lifted him from the floor, then carried him as though he were a rolled-up blanket, one arm under his shoulders and the other under his knees. The man supported his weight quite easily, and smiled placidly at Cora and said, "The room key?"

"It's in his pocket," she said. "His trousers pocket."

"Good," the man said. He widened the smile just a trifle. "Don't look so worried. He's all right."

She didn't say anything.

"He's quite all right," the man said. "He's doing fine now."

Bevan mumbled something in his sleep. He squirmed in the man's arms. The man went on smiling at Cora and said, "He needs a pillow under his head. That's all he needs."

"Then why don't you take him upstairs? What are you waiting for?"

The man's eyebrows went up just a little, but the smile stayed on his lips.

"I'm sorry," Cora murmured. "I shouldn't have put it that way."

"Oh, that's all right," the man said lightly. "It's understandable."

Then he turned away and carried the drunken
sleeper out of the bar and across the lobby and toward
the row of elevators. At the doorway between bar and
lobby, Cora stood watching him as he waited with his
burden for the elevator. She was thinking, Whoever
he is, he's a brute. Very polite and considerate and
completely a brute. Look at him, how big he is. Look
at his shoulders. Such wide shoulders. He's so much
bigger than the man he's carrying. That's what he
wants me to know. That's why he stood there smiling at
me, drilling it into me that he's bigger, he's bigger and
better. Next thing he'll want to do is show me his hairy
chest. Does he have a hairy chest? Why do you ask? I
don't know. Then stop asking. But does he really have
a hairy chest? And will you please stop trembling? But
it isn't trembling. It's shivering. Yes, you're shivering,
you feel so cold, so terribly cold. But there's a furnace
somewhere, it's coming nearer, it's very hot, it's white-
hot coming nearer and nearer, but no, it isn't a furnace,
it's a hand, it's a man's hand. It's the hand of...

Of whom? Of what?

There was no answer to that, and she thought. It's
nothing, really. It's just a momentary lapse. You know
you can get rid of it if you try because you've had this
sort of thing before and you've always managed to get
rid of it. But what is it? Why does it happen?

She stood rigidly, watching the man as he entered
the elevator with the sleeping burden slung across his
arms. Then the elevator door was closed and she
looked up to the floor indicator and saw the pointer
moving slowly toward two and past two and toward

three. It stopped at three. Her eyes were focused on the numeral three engraved in the bronze of the floor indicator. Three, she thought. What's the meaning of three? There's a saying, three little words. There's another saying, three's a crowd. There's also the arithmetic we learn in first grade and it tells us that three and three are six and three are nine. And what's the meaning of nine?

I'll tell you what the meaning is, she said to herself. You're thinking the way a child thinks. A child who is nine years old. Please try to remember you're grown up, you're twenty years older than nine years old... nine years old...nine years old...

She shivered again. It was a convulsive shiver and in the moment that it lasted there was the coldness and then the awful heat changing shape and becoming a man's hand. She took a backward step to get away from it, then another backward step, and her hands came up to her eyes, her palms pressing hard against her eyes so that what she saw was blackness. It was a thick and greasy and terribly filthy blackness, it was like the dark of a sewer that went down and down and now she could feel the wetness and she knew where it was. She tried to believe it wasn't there but it was there. It was actually there, the seething hot wetness that caused her to gasp and groan without sound.

So it's happened, she thought. It's happened again. It hasn't happened for quite a while now but tonight something brought it on, although we're agreed the circumstances are quite different from that last time, more than a year ago, that rainy afternoon when you couldn't get a taxi and you used the subway. It was during the rush hour and the car was packed and you were standing next to that big man wearing the ship-yard worker's helmet. He was so big, so ugly, and his shirt was unbuttoned and you saw the hair on his chest. What a horrible-looking beast he was, and he saw you were looking at him, and it was as though he knew what you were thinking. Or what you didn't know you were thinking. Because he grinned at you as though to say, "You ain't kidding me, girlie. On the outside you looked scared stiff, really freezing-scared. But inside you're on fire." Was it true? Of course it was true. First thing I did when I got home was take a hot bath. I think that's what I'll do tonight. I'll take a hot bath. But you don't need a bath, you had one just an hour ago. You really don't need a bath. Oh, don't you? Not much you don't. You feel as though you haven't bathed for a week. Oh, this is such an awful mess. I wish there were some kind of soap that washes out the mind.

She walked across the lobby and seated herself in an armchair with her back to the elevator doors. A few minutes passed and then she heard the action of the elevator door as it opened. She was slumped low in the chair and she was hoping he wouldn't see her, then hoping he would see her, and then hoping he wouldn't see her.

He didn't see her. She heard the heavy footsteps of his thick-soled shoes under his bulky weight, moving across the lobby in the other direction, going toward the bar. She turned her head and caught a glimpse of him as he entered the bar, seeing him in profile, his close-curled carrot-colored hair and slightly flattened nose and thick shoulders and bulging chest. Then he was out of sight, but in her mind she sensed the brute force of his presence moving toward her and she shivered again.

The elevator door remained open and she got up and hurried toward it. In Room 307 she undressed quickly, in a hurry to get into the tub. But as she started toward the bathroom, she glanced at the twin bed where the drunken sleeper was flat on his back. His leg was bent over the side of the bed at what appeared to be an uncomfortable angle. She lifted his leg, getting his foot onto the bed, and as she did this the look on her face was wifely and tender. She stood there gazing at him and sighing, and thinking, It isn't his fault he drinks so much. It's your fault. You know it's your fault. At moments such as this you understand clearly and completely that it's your fault. You're his burden and his grief, you're the living puzzle that he can't solve. Why don't you give him the answer?

You can't give him the answer. Because there's no answer to give. You wish you knew the answer. Oh, how you wish it would come to you, or at least come close enough so you could reach out and make a grab for it. But it's very far away, this certain answer, this dancing joker of an answer that tells the why and wherefore of all these twisted, strangled, anguished years.

How many years?

When did it happen?

When did what happen? What was it? You have no

idea what it was. Whatever it was, it must have been something on the dreadful side. It must have been so shockingly dreadful that you couldn't tell anyone. You must have said to yourself, Not a living soul must know. So you had it buried inside yourself, buried deep and then deeper and finally drifting down and away from all known depth of memory. I guess that's what you wanted it to do. You wanted it to go away, you wished to forget all about it. The wish was granted and here you are just like the little girl who tosses away her toy balloon, and as it soars away she wants it to come back, but of course it won't come back.

Toy balloon. Little girl. Is that a clue?

Not really. But let's stay with little girl. What are little girls made of?

Sugar and spice and everything nice. That's what Mother always said. She told you to remember it always, to keep yourself dainty and neat, and most important of all, don't get yourself dirty. You can hear her saying it again: "All right, go out in the garden and play, but don't get yourself dirty."

Dirty. That reminds me, I ought to start the water running in the tub. But you don't need a bath. Oh, yes, you do. You need plenty of soap and water, little girl. You must—

But wait now. The garden. What about the garden? I remember, we lived in that big house on Long Island and there was a very large garden and I was seven or eight or nine years old or maybe five or six or eleven. If only I could remember…Yes, if only you could remember. But of course your only memory is Mother saying, "Don't get yourself dirty."

But the garden, I think there was something in the garden....

The flowers? What flowers? No, it wasn't the flowers. Was it that thing made of marble? The bird bath? No, it wasn't the bird bath. What else was there? Some kind of pond, I think. A small pond. It was very small, a fish pond. Yes, I remember now it was a goldfish pond.

Goldfish pond. Goldfish pond. Keep saying it. Please keep saying it. I think it means something. I'm sure it does. Oh, it must mean something. In connection with what? With whom? With whose face? Whose voice?

I can't remember. The only voice I remember is the voice of Mother saying, "Don't get yourself dirty."

She went in to the bathroom and started the hot water running in the tub.

Chapter Two

He stayed in bed until well past noon. His stomach felt awful and his throat burned. A colored girl came up with a tray and he tried to get some food down, but he gagged on it and said that what he really needed was another drink. The girl went out and some minutes later came back with a double whisky and a small pitcher of ice water. The whisky lifted him a little and he told the girl to bring him a bottle and a large pitcher. But as the girl started out he changed his mind and said, "Let's see if I can hold off till tonight."

Then the girl was gone and he was alone in the room. He wondered where Cora was. Then he told himself it didn't matter where she was or what she was doing. For a while he sat there in the bed, smoking cigarettes and looking at the opened window, wishing a breeze would come in. It was terribly hot in here. It was the middle of February and he thought of them freezing in New York while here in Jamaica it was well over ninety. A ribbon of blinding-yellow Caribbean sunlight slashed across the pale-yellow percale that covered his upraised knees. Then something else came through the window and it was a mosaic of quietly pleasant sound from down below, in and around the swimming pool. He climbed out of bed and walked to the window and looked out.

He saw them down there, the American and British

tourists wearing sunglasses and carefully selected beach attire. Even from this distance one could tell they were people of means and good breeding. They were having fun down there and it was clean quiet fun; there were no show-offs on the diving board, no pseudo acrobats on the sand, no scanty bathing suits. The chatter and laughter was tempered, blending with the serene design of the pool and its surroundings. Altogether it was a placid scene of nice placid people enjoying themselves. He wanted to put on his bathing trunks and go down there and get in on it.

And yet, as he gazed down from the opened window, he knew there was something wrong with the picture. What you mean is, he thought, there's something wrong with this party looking at the picture. This party doesn't belong in that setting. That setting is strictly for sober-minded individuals who know how to behave themselves. And this party here, this weak-kneed, weak-brained gin-head—oh, yes, this perfect example of self-ruination, this absolute failure—

"Oh, screw that noise," he muttered aloud. But the sound of his own voice, burned with gin and twisted with anguish, made dismal contrast with the gay care-free sounds from the pool and sand and garden down below. He moved away from the window, noticed the radio on the small table set between the twin beds. He turned on the radio and listened to a calypso singer complaining to the neighbors that they should stop stealing from his kitchen, his wife was getting too skinny. It wasn't very good calypso.

There were some ten minutes more of calypso, then

a station break, and then the broadcast of a cricket match between Jamaicans and a team from England. The announcer was very technical and Bevan had very little knowledge of cricket and had no idea what the man was talking about. But he stood there and listened anyway, trying to follow it, trying to aim his mind at the cricket players and away from himself.

"A truly splendid score," the announcer said. "For Baxter it's now—"

Good for Baxter, he said without sound as the score was stated. But not at all good for Bevan. Let's try another cigarette. No, that won't improve matters. Let's try a cold shower.

He showered and shaved and put on his clothes. Then he took them off and got into his bathing trunks. Then he took off the trunks and put on his clothes again. He tied his shoelaces slowly at first, fumbling with the laces, then suddenly very quickly and instinctively because his brain was aimed at something else he had to do.

He had to take another look out that window.

At the window he aimed his eyes at what he'd seen before but hadn't wanted to notice. Delayed reaction, he thought, focusing on the pale-orange bathing suit she wore, her pale-yellow hair glimmering almost white under the scorching sun. She was sitting in a beach chair near the edge of the swimming pool and without sound he said, Hello Cora. He saw her turning her head, saying something to the man who sat in the adjoining beach chair. Without sound Bevan said,

Hello, Flatnose, but he knew the nickname was an exaggeration; the man's nose was not that flat. He tried Carrot-top, but that didn't seem proper, either. The carrot-colored hair was somewhat on the darkish side, not the flaring red-orange that would automatically label one a carrot-top. And anyway, he told himself, the name isn't important. What's important is the fact that there they are, sitting next to each other. And look at her now, look at the way she's smiling at him. Now he's saying something and she's paying very close attention.

Tell you what, you better go down there and break it up before it starts. Or maybe it's started already. Yes, you might as well admit it's started already. It got started last night when he moved in to lend a hand, gallantly aiding the tearful lady who couldn't manage her drunken husband. Well, that's the way it happens sometimes. And in this case it was bound to happen sooner or later. It certainly stands to reason she'd come across a Someone Else. Or make it Mr. Something who moves in to replace Mr. Zero. That sounds logical, it's altogether functional. All right, let's stop it right there.

But look at them; they're not stopping it. Look how interested she is. She can't take her eyes off him. You can actually measure the vibration between them. Or is it merely something you're imagining? No, I don't think so. It's a decisive vibration, it's like an ache that throbs and throbs and it's getting worse. If it doesn't stop...

*

If it doesn't stop, Cora was thinking, I'm afraid something will happen. I know something will happen. But
of course it's happening already and there's no way to
break it off, unless I just get up from this beach chair
and walk away from him. I can't do that. Why can't
you? Well, it wouldn't be right. It would be terribly
rude, outrageously rude. But that isn't the answer. The
answer is that you're chained to this chair, you can't
move.

She was sitting there in the beach chair next to the
heavily built man whose nose was slightly flattened,
whose hair was carrot-colored, who sat with his legs
crossed so that his thickly muscled thighs bulged
prominently. His only attire was navy-blue swimming
shorts and navy-blue leather sandals. His bare chest
was very hairy and there was considerable hair on his
arms and on the backs of his large hands. He had very
large hands and he used them with moderate expres-
siveness while he talked.

He was talking about the theatre. He was telling her
about a very fine performance of Ibsen he'd recently
seen in New York. He said that Bankhead was really
wonderful when she was doing Ibsen, and of course
Le Gallienne was always superlative, and then he included Cornell and Nazimova. But the greatest of
Ibsen he'd ever seen, he said, was Bankhead doing
Hedda Gabbler.

"I saw it on television," Cora said.

"Did it get across?"

"It was all right."

"I wouldn't want to see it on television. If I'm going to see it, I want to see it on the stage. And no further back than the fourth row."

"And if you can't get the fourth row?"

"Oh, I get it," he said. "When I want it badly enough, I always manage to get it."

It was quiet for some moments and then he went on talking about Ibsen. He compared Ibsen with some of the moderns and he said a few of the moderns were quite good but not really up there with Ibsen. The way he put it, he said these moderns kept using left jabs and sometimes they managed to rock you with a right to the jaw. But it took Ibsen to smash you so hard that you were knocked flat. He said it was the same feeling that came from hearing a record of the voice of John McCormack. He had a great many records by John McCormack, and another favorite of his was Chaliapin. He stated emphatically that none of the modern singers could approach those two.

For a while he talked about singers and then he came back to Ibsen, but now she couldn't follow what he was saying. She sat there looking directly at him but not hearing the words that came from his mouth, hearing only the sound of his voice, which was thick and rumbling and seemed to be closing in on her like thunder approaching from all directions. And then, all at once, she forgot who he was.

She forgot that he'd said his name was Atkinson and that his home was in New York and whatever else he'd mentioned about himself. Now it was as though he had no identity; he was just a big man with a rough-textured face and a hairy chest and large hands. She looked at his hands, which were scrubbed spotless, the fingernails neatly trimmed and buffed. She tried to stop looking at his hands but she couldn't stop looking and now her brain was a screen that showed the hands moving toward her, the fingers clawing, the hands now grimy, the fingernails blackened and filthy. There was the far-off echo of a voice that said to her: "You can't get away. He's so big—he's so rough...."

When did you hear that? she asked herself. And who said it? Then the voice spoke again. It said, "Please don't. Oh, please don't." It was such a tiny voice, like the pleading chirping of a frightened little bird. Or a child, she thought. A girl-child. Yes, a very little girl, let's say seven or eight or nine years old. Can you be more specific? No, and it's no use trying. And leave me alone, she said to herself.

She heard him saying, "—is probably the trouble with the theatre these days. Don't you agree?"

She nodded mechanically.

He smiled and said, "I'm sorry, Mrs. Bevan. I didn't mean to interrupt."

"Interrupt what?"

"Whatever it was you were thinking about."

She smiled back at him. "It wasn't anything important." And then, apologetically, "You must think I'm awfully impolite."

"Not at all," and he laughed lightly. "You just went away for a moment and then you came back."

She laughed with him. She was thinking, You're all

right now. You're just sitting here making conversation. That's all it is, it's nothing more than a pleasant conversation.

Bevan stood there at the window, watching them. Then gradually and for some unaccountable reason his attention was drawn away and he was focusing on the yellow-brown stone wall beyond the far side of the swimming pool. It was a high wall and it marked the line of separation between the Laurel Rock Hotel and the native dwellings. Now he was looking out and over the fence wall and he had a clear view. He could see the narrow streets crowded with dark-skinned people who either sat motionless on doorsteps or moved listlessly, seeming to have nothing special to do and no special place to go. They were too far away for him to check their attire, but he received the impression that most of them wore rags, and he saw many of them walking barefoot. There were some women carrying baskets on their heads, their hands not touching the baskets, their legs and torsos moving in a steady rhythm that balanced the baskets, and it amounted to an art. He remembered the travel folder that had played it up big: "See the colorful native women who carry baskets on their heads." Except that in the travel folder the baskets were filled with flowers and the women wore a lot of jewelry and trinkets and bright-hued dresses, grinning brightly and happily from the glossy page. He told himself there was little or no similarity between the travel folder and what he was seeing now. These women wore no jewelry, and the

dresses looked like something made from flour bags.
The baskets on their heads contained no flowers, only
food, and even from this distance he could see the
blackness on the skins of the bananas. He thought
technically, They better hurry and sell that fruit. It'll
soon get spoiled in the sun.

He watched a flock of naked children racing across
a garbage-littered back yard that faced the harbor.
They came onto a splintered, deserted pier and leaped
feet first into the scummy water. He saw them swimming out toward cleaner, bluer water where a large
cabin cruiser was anchored. They were hoping to
attract some attention and then go diving for tossed
pennies. Without realizing what he was doing, Bevan
put his hand in his pocket, reaching for coins. As he
felt the silver between his fingers he said to himself,
It's only a phony gesture.

You sure have a gift for that. You're a first-rate
performer when it comes to making phony gestures. If
you want to look back and examine the record, you'll
see just how dismally phony. But you better not do
that; you better not look back. If you do, you'll require
another drink, a great many drinks. So please don't do
it, please don't allow yourself to remember.

His eyes went on aiming at the slum area on the
other side of the hotel wall. But the scene reflected on
the screen of his mind had nothing to do with the city
of Kingston on the island of Jamaica. It was another
slum area, located in Manhattan. Around Fiftieth Street
and Tenth Avenue.

Some two years ago. Or was it three?

Stop it, he begged himself.

But his brain said, No, you can't stop it. You've tried so many times, but there's no set of brakes for this kind of action. Once it starts, it keeps on going, with the gears in reverse and the wheels rolling downhill past all the used-up calendars.

His head went down. He slumped into a chair near the window. There was a dazed and stricken look on his face as he surrendered himself to the tides of memory.

It begins, he told himself, with a sleepless night.

But that wasn't it, not really. He knew it actually began with his marriage to Cora. It had seemed like a proper marriage, properly romantic and with all the proper factors of mutual respect and tenderness and affection. During the seven months of their engagement their only physical contact had been when they danced and when they kissed. Of course he wanted to do more than that, but he'd made a firm resolve not to try. He knew he was marrying a girl who hadn't been around, a girl of better-than-average breeding and background, her chastity a precious truth that needed no words, because it showed in her eyes. So he forced himself to wait until the wedding night, anticipating that the wedding night would be sweetly magical and wonderful.

The wedding night was miserable. She sobbed, "It's horrible. I can't—I just can't." It went on like that through the honeymoon, and later it fell into the

dreary pattern of an ordeal for her and little or no
pleasure for him. Of course, she tried, she really tried,
but that only made it worse. He developed the guilty
knowledge that he was forcing her to do something
she didn't want to do, hated to do. And what made it
tougher on him was that she never wanted to talk
about it. One night she wept terribly and begged him
to be patient with her, and he bit hard at the side of his
mouth to keep from exclaiming impatiently. She said
she'd keep on trying, but it wasn't long after that she
suggested they purchase twin beds.

"But why?"

"Well—I know it's difficult for you. I mean—"

"Yes, I know what you mean."

"I'm sorry, James. I'm awfully sorry."

"It's all right," he said. He managed to smile at her.
"Don't let it worry you, dear. It isn't anything to worry
about."

But during the first three years he worried plenty.
Then gradually he became accustomed to the twice-a-
month routine and later the once-a-month routine. He
was working very hard on Wall Street, and weekends
he concentrated on his golf, so at night he was more or
less played out, really anxious for sleep and nothing
but sleep. In the fifth year of their marriage she
became pregnant and for a time he thought that might
change matters; the doctor told him that after a woman
has her first child she becomes aroused, becomes a
hungry female animal fully aware of her gender.

That never happened because in the seventh month
she had a miscarriage. Two years later she had another

miscarriage and for several months thereafter she was very sick. The doctor said she was too narrow in the hips, and recommended that she put on weight before attempting another pregnancy. During her convalescence she gained a few pounds, but she lost it just as soon as she was back on her feet. One night she climbed into his bed and put her arms around him and said, "You want me?"

"Sure," he said. "I always want you."

But as he hugged her, his fingers caressing her fragile shoulders, he could feel she was trembling, and he sensed the effort she was making, forcing herself to give him what he needed. He told himself she was a good girl, she was sweet and generous and he was awfully lucky to have her for a wife. What followed after that was a stab of guilt that told him he had hurt her enough with his animal requirements and he mustn't hurt her any more. But Jesus Christ, he thought, I'm flesh and blood, and I need it, I've got to have it, and what am I to do? All right, I know it's a wonderful marriage from the standpoint of how much I care for her. I really adore this girl. Christ, I don't know what I'd do without her, she's so good, so sweet. Yes, she's my life, she's the soft violin music that makes it all worth living, the delicate pastel creature that makes every other creature unimportant. Oh, yes, she's the softly murmured poetry that shuts out all the blatant sounds of a too-loud city, a too-busy world. So what she offers me is the placid world where I see her adorable face and listen to her adorable voice. That's what I cherish, and it ought to be enough.

And the point is, mister, it isn't enough.

He heard Cora murmuring, "Now—please, dear. Now."

But what she's actually saying is: Hurry and let's get it over with. Like when you were in Yale and every now and then you'd hit some joint in New Haven and pay your five dollars and the girl would say, "Let's speed it up, college boy, I got more customers waiting." You could laugh about that, and perhaps if you were sufficiently philosophical you could laugh about this. But I don't think this is a laughing matter. No, it's definitely not a laughing matter. For seven years you've been married to an extremely sweet and exceptionally pretty girl, and that's one side of it. The other side is the fact that for some goddamn reason she can't respond to your maleness. Let's face it, you know that in all the times we've done it she's never had an orgasm. It's as though she were something made of wax. Or ice.

"James?" There was a slight quiver of impatience in her voice.

"Listen, dear, I'd rather—"

"You'd rather what?"

"Well, I'm awfully tired. Really knocked out."

There was a long stillness. And then she said, "You're not angry?"

"Angry?" He managed a lightly incredulous laugh. "What are you talking about? Why should I be angry?"

"Because I—" But she couldn't go on with it. She sighed heavily and said, "Oh, thank you for being so patient with me. You're so good to me, James."

"We're good to each other," he said. "I guess it's because we like each other."

"Yes, we do like each other very much. It's so nice to know that. We really admire each other, and I think that's awfully important, don't you?"

"Uh-huh." And then he pretended a yawn.

"Poor dear," she whispered. "You're so tired. I'll let you get some sleep."

She went back to her own bed. He was flat on his back, his eyes open, looking up at the blackness of the ceiling. In a little while he heard the steady deep rhythm of her breathing, and he knew she was asleep.

He didn't know that his eyes were narrowing. He didn't sense the approach of the invisible reptile sliding toward his mind. The reptile was an idea that touched him ever so lightly and whispered, You need it, you need it bad, and you can't get it here—but maybe you can get it somewhere else.

No, he said to the slimy thing. And get away from me.

You fool, you, the reptile said.

Get away. Get out of here. You're rotten. You smell bad.

Maybe so, the reptile said. But aside from that, I'm your friend. I'm giving you good advice.

Take it somewhere else. I'm not interested.

Not much. You're all ears, brother. For seven years you've put up with this misery, this living with a woman who has little or no heat, who just can't respond the way she ought to respond. So what it amounts to is seven years of frustration. I think it's about time you did something about it.

Like what?

Come with me, the reptile said.

It was in him, coiled tightly around his nerves. It dragged him out of bed, telling him to move very quietly so as not to wake her up. Some moonlight came through the window, and in the silver-blue glow he put on his clothes, pausing to glance at the luminous face of the alarm clock on the dresser. The hands pointed to twenty minutes past twelve.

He told himself she was a sound sleeper and she wouldn't open her eyes until the alarm went off at seven in the morning. By that time he'd be back in bed. That much he knew for sure. There was the slightest trace of a smile on his lips as he walked out of the apartment and down the corridor toward the elevator.

The elevator lowered him eleven floors to street level. It was only a short walk to Lexington Avenue, and in less than a minute he was climbing into a taxi.

"Where to?" the driver asked.

He didn't say anything.

The driver turned and looked at him. The taxi was stopped for a red light and in the pinkish glow he saw the questioning frown on the driver's face.

He said, "I'm not sure. I'm wondering where to go."

"Oh," the driver said. A pause drifted in and became sort of meaningful, and then the driver murmured, "You jes wanna go for a ride? Is that it?"

"Not exactly."

"You mean you wanna go someplace but you don't know where it is? Izzat what you're trying to say?"

"Something on that order."

The driver took a closer look at the man in the back seat. "You wanna talk some business?" he asked.

"All right."

"How much you think it's worth for me to take you there?"

"I wouldn't know."

"Things are tight in this town right now," the driver said. "They got a drive on. For me it's a gamble, I guess you know that?"

"Is ten dollars all right?"

"That'll make it," the driver said.

It was a small dingy taproom on Tenth Avenue near Fiftieth Street. The driver went in, telling him to wait in the taxi. A few minutes later the driver came out and said she was sitting alone in a booth, she was the one in the green dress.

He gave the driver a ten-dollar bill and two ones for a tip, and entered the taproom. At the bar there were some unshaven men who looked like truck drivers or longshoremen. There was a fat shapeless woman with gray hair drinking beer with a little Spanish-looking man whose clothes needed pressing. In one of the booths there were a couple of very young sailors sitting with girls. In another booth there were a few middle-aged women, two of them wearing mannish haircuts and checked shirts and dungarees. He moved past them, past several empty booths, and came to where she was sitting alone, her dress a very bright green against the drab gray-brown of the unvarnished booth.

She was sort of skinny, but it wasn't the broomstick build. It wasn't brittle or dried up; it certainly wasn't the cheap-whore skinniness. The lines of her body amounted to a price tag saying, costs more than the average. And her face showed it, too. She had a nice face, not ornamental or prettily nice, but she could certainly model for the serious painters who preferred to emphasize depth. She had black hair and black-brown eyes and a serious mouth that told him she did more thinking than talking. They had a few drinks. While they drank, they smoked his cigarettes and said very little. What it amounted to, she had a room on Fiftieth just around the corner, and if he cared to put in some time there, her price was fifteen dollars. The way she said it, he knew it was the flat rate, there'd be no haggling. And yet her tone was more friendly than professional. Somehow she didn't seem professional. She told him she was French and Portuguese and her name was Lita and she had three children living with her sister in Baltimore. She was willing to talk more about that, but his anxiousness showed and she said, "Come on, I'll show ya my room."

She gave him a nice time. There was something about it that made him forget it was a business arrangement. He'd paid her in advance, so that took care of that, and what followed was all physical activity, extremely enjoyable because it seemed there was nothing forced or mechanical in what she was doing. It seemed that every move she made was aimed at getting the utmost of pleasure from him, as though he represented a kind of opportunity that didn't come along very often and she wanted to make the most of it while it lasted.

When it was finished he didn't want to leave. He looked in his wallet and saw there were only nine dollars there. She said nine dollars would be all right for now and he could pay her the six he owed when he came back next time. So he stayed with her some forty minutes longer.

While he was getting dressed she said, "You got money for taxi fare?"

He smiled somewhat sheepishly and shook his head. "Here, take this," she said, putting a five-dollar bill in his hand.

He murmured, "It's awfully nice of you."

She shrugged and didn't say anything. They walked out together and she went into the taproom to wait for another customer. On the corner of Tenth Avenue and Fiftieth he stopped a taxi and went home.

A few nights later he was with her again. It became a pattern of seeing her twice a week, and that went on for a couple of months. After that it was three times a week. One night he kiddingly suggested that she give him a special rate. She looked at him and said, quite seriously, "I been thinking about it. I mean, maybe we can arrange something."

"It's all right," he said. "I was just joking."

"No, I think ya meant it," she said quietly and more seriously. "After all, this is costing ya lotsa good cabbage. Never less than thirty bucks a night, and some nights ya pay me forty-five. That's not counting the drinks ya sport for us in Hallihan's. Of course, if ya can afford it—"

"Sure, I can afford it." But just then it occurred to him that he certainly couldn't afford it. He frowned slightly and she went on looking at him.

They were quiet for some moments and then she said, "Well, whaddaya say? Ya wanna set me up?"

He didn't know what she meant by that. He smiled the question at her. The smile mixed with a frown.

She said, "Ya know ya can't afford it the way it is now. Ya don't make that much loot. I figure ya for maybe ten grand a year, maybe a little more."

"That's a fair estimate," he admitted. He went on with the mixed smile and frown, trying to get rid of the frown. And now he wasn't looking at her.

He heard her saying, "I think I gotcha figured, George. Of course, I know yer name ain't really George, that's one thing. But that's all right, ya wanna be George, yer George. I gotcha listed like say around thirty-five and married and ya live in a nice apartment with maid service and when yer wife gets her hair done it's never less than ten bucks a throw. Correct?"

"Just about," he murmured absently. "I think she pays the hairdresser seven-fifty."

"Ya don't care what she pays. Anything she does is all right with you."

The frown deepened. He wondered why she'd said that. He wondered why he couldn't look at her. He said, "What are you doing, Lita? You fishing for information?"

"Not exactly. The way it is now, it ain't none of my business. But even so, there's certain things I know without ya putting me wise. Not that I been making investigations. I don't go in for that crap. It's just that some whores can get to know someone just from cruising him. For example, ya never said a word about it, but I know it bothers ya I got other customers."

He didn't say anything.

She went on: "I might as well tell ya that makes a hit with me. I mean ya keeping it to yerself because ya felt ya didn't have no right to mention it. As a matter of fact, George, there's a lotta angles about ya that makes ya sorta special in my book. Or maybe I don't hafta tell ya that. I guess ya know."

He looked at her. He wasn't frowning now. He wasn't smiling, either. "You're an awfully nice person, Lita."

"Not all the time," she said. "Sometimes I'm just plain mean and salty. But I try to be nice when people are nice to me. Like with you, for instance. Like last week when ya staked me to them earrings, like a coupla weeks ago, that box of candy. It wasn't cheap candy, neither. Look, I'll tell ya something, George. I'm ready for ya to set me up—if ya wanna, that is. I'm ready to give up the other customers. You'll be the only thing in pants coming into this room. How's that sound?"

"It sounds fine—" But he said it without enthusiasm.

She gave him a side glance. She frowned slightly.

And he said, "What I mean is, it sounds fine to me. But what about you? You'll be losing out financially."

"Don't let that bother ya," she said. "I can get along on whatever ya give me each week. Wanna make it sixty? Fifty?"

"Let's make it seventy."

"Ya can't afford seventy."

"I think I can just about manage it."

"Tell ya what," she cut in quickly. "Let's make it sixty and see how it works out."

"All right," he said.

And then he reached for his wallet to pay her in advance for their session tonight. But as he took out the ten and the five she shook her head and said, "You're not a customer now. You're my—"

"Your boyfriend?" He smiled.

"Hey now." She grinned. "My boyfriend. That sounds swell." She started to take off her clothes. As she unzipped her skirt she said, "Tonight the drinks are on me. I'm celebrating. I got me a good-looking boyfriend."

It worked out very nicely. Every Monday night he handed her sixty dollars. He always met her in Hallihan's on Tenth Avenue and they would have a few drinks and then go to the room. It was never less than three nights a week and some weeks he'd manage to find an hour or so in the afternoon between business appointments. All he had to do was phone Hallihan's and they'd tell her when he was due to arrive. They were very cooperative at Hallihan's, and the bartenders and the regulars always minded their own business. Aside from giving him an amiable smile or an offhand "Hiya, George, how ya doin'?" they never bothered him, and they made it a point to keep their distance when he was there with Lita. It was as though he had their unspoken approval, as though they were pleased that Lita had discarded her profession to be his steady girlfriend.

Another thing that made it nice, there was no problem with Cora, for the simple and somehow amazing reason that Cora didn't know. At times he could scarcely believe it, but the fact remained that he'd managed to hide it from her. Of course, it needed a flock of untruths, like telling her about late-at-night business appointments, or customer prospects out of town. She never questioned these explanations. Her only comment was "You're working so hard these days—these nights, I mean."

And he found it easy to reply with a smile, "I don't mind it, honey. It agrees with me."

She smiled back easily and pleasantly and said, "All right, Mr. Businessman. You're the boss. Only thing is, I'm worried you don't get enough sleep."

So it was altogether a nice setup and it went on that way for five months. What ruined it was early one Sunday morning after he'd been with Lita most of Saturday night he came back to the apartment and Cora was sitting up in bed reading a magazine. He stared at the cover of the magazine. It was *Harper's Bazaar*. He said, "Why aren't you sleeping?"

Without taking her eyes from the page she said, "I found out, James. I followed you last night."

He went on staring at the cover of *Harper's Bazaar*. It showed a young lady wearing a chinchilla coat leaning against one of the stone lions in front of the Fifth Avenue library. He heard Cora saying, "I'm sorry, James. I guess it's my fault."

Quickly he said, "No, don't say that."

But she went on: "Yes, I know it's my fault. I can't provide you with what you need. I really can't blame you for seeking it somewhere else."

On the magazine cover the stone lion looked at him and said without sound, You two-timing sonofabitch, you're getting off easy. Then he saw Cora looking at him and she was saying, "What do you want me to do, James? Do you want me to leave?"

He said, "No, don't do that. Please don't do that."

She gave him a pathetic smile, the pathos meant for both of them. "Why not?" she asked quietly. "You have this other woman. You certainly don't need me."

He shut his eyes very tightly and kept them shut for a long moment. Then, looking at her directly and keeping his voice steady, he said, "I do need you. And there's no other woman. That was just something that happened. It was a mistake and I'm sorry and I won't let it happen again."

Next day he broke it off with Lita. It was in the afternoon. He phoned Hallihan's and they called her to the phone. Before he said anything she asked him what was wrong. He wanted to say there was nothing wrong and he'd be seeing her tonight. Instead he said, "My wife found out about it. I guess you know what that means."

Lita didn't say anything.

He said, "It means we can't see each other any more."

There was no sound at the other end of the wire.

"Listen." He swallowed hard. "Listen, Lita, I'm terribly sorry. You don't know how sorry I am."

Then he waited for her to say something but there was still no sound.

He said, "I hope you'll try to understand."

And again he waited. And finally she said, "It's O.K., George. Don't let it getcha down."

Well, now, he thought. This is certainly rougher than I thought it would be. Then he heard himself saying, "I'm mailing you a money order for—" But he stopped there because it seemed very much out of place; it sounded cheap.

And she was saying, "No, don't do that. For Christ's sake, don't send me any money. I might as well tell ya, George—it wasn't the money. It was— Oh, well, we'll skip that. But—" She faltered and tried again and faltered, then finally got it out: "I'm sure gonna miss ya."

He closed his eyes. He wished he had a bottle with him so he could take a hefty drink. It was the first time in his life he'd actually craved a drink. But that didn't occur to him just then. Just then the only thing he knew was that he needed a bracer.

He was concentrating on the need for a drink and didn't realize she was giving him a break when she said goodbye very quickly and hung up. He replaced the receiver on the hook, stepped out of the booth, made a fast exit from the drugstore, and went across the street to a bar, where he ordered a double shot of bonded bourbon. In the weeks that followed he gradually managed to put Lita out of his mind. Or rather, he gradually erased the thought pictures that showed her taking her clothes off, then sitting on the edge of the bed with her hands resting on her bare thighs. The picture that stayed in his brain the longest was of Lita with nothing on, leaning her elbow against the wall near the bed, standing there with her hand drowned in the dark hair that fell loosely onto her thin shoulders. The wall was a dark gray and her body was cream-yellow against the darkness. She was awfully skinny but it was a flexible construction, it was soft and somehow electric-wild, the voltage charging across to him where he reclined on the bed looking at her, getting hit with the blaze that never failed to blast him thrillingly whenever she stood there with nothing on.

When that picture was gone, he tried to pay physical attention to Cora. But of course it couldn't work: there was nothing there to work with. It was the same as it had always been, with Cora seemingly attempting to do the best she could, with her gasps and groans the sounds of forced and painful effort instead of head-bursting pleasure. The sounds she made were downright pitiful, and more than once he felt so much pity that he couldn't continue with it, he had to let go of her. In the instant that his arms fell away, letting her know it was postponed tonight and he'd take a rain check on it, he heard her gasping again. Only now it was more of a sigh. It was a sigh of relief.

So that was the way it was in the bedroom with

Cora. He put up with it for nine weeks and ten weeks and in the middle of the eleventh week he couldn't stand it any longer. He remembered now it was a Thursday night with the alarm clock showing one-fifteen, with Cora sound asleep in the other bed and himself wide awake staring at the green numbers on the face of the clock. The green became active, its circular phosphorescence coiling out from the face of the clock like a reptile emerging from a hole. Then it crawled toward him and into him and he climbed out of bed and started to get dressed.

Some thirty minutes later a taxi dropped him off at the corner of Fiftieth Street and Tenth Avenue.

He walked into Hallihan's and went up to the bar. There weren't many customers in the place. He saw a sprinkling of the regulars, the little Spanish-looking man whose clothes needed pressing, the fat shapeless gray-haired woman drinking beer, a few middle-aged Teamsters Union organizers wearing their union buttons, and one of the booths contained two worried-looking men who wore sharp-cut suits of cheap fabric and gave the impression that they'd just emerged with empty pockets from a floating crap game. Another booth had a lone occupant, a beefy blonde pug-nosed woman, heavily painted and obviously a professional looking for a customer. The bartender stood there waiting for his order and he asked for a bonded bourbon. The bartender poured it, rang up the sale and gave him his change, and started to move away. He said, "Hold it, Mike."

The bartender turned and looked at him.

He said, "What is it, Mike? What's the matter?"

The bartender shrugged and didn't say anything.

"Don't you remember me?" he asked, smiling.

"Sure," the bartender said. "Sure, I gotcha checked."

He let the smile drift away. He knew the smile was useless, it wasn't doing any good at all. And then, in the quiet that seemed to thicken and close in like fog, he sensed that the other drinkers were looking at him.

He heard the bartender say, "Anything on your mind?"

"I'm looking for Lita."

"She ain't around," the bartender said.

"Can you tell me where she is?"

"Sure," the bartender said. "She's in the cemetery."

The quiet became very thick and it pressed against him. He had the feeling it would crush him if he didn't break through it and say something.

He said, "Tell me, Mike."

"Sure, I'll tell you," the bartender said. His voice was louder now, somewhat oratorical, as though he wanted all the others to hear. "She went to pieces, that's what happened. She hit the bottle like I never seen it hit before. We kicked her out so many times I lost count. But that didn't do no good. If she couldn't get it here, she'd get it somewhere else. So one night a coupla weeks ago she's plastered and trying to make it across Tenth Avenue and a big truck comes along. The driver claimed she walked right into the headlights."

"You mean she—"

"I mean she was plastered, that's all. She was plastered stiff and she didn't know where she was going."

Then it was quiet again. But now the quiet was thin and there was no pressure, there was nothing.

"You feel bad about it?" the bartender asked.

He didn't reply.

"You oughta feel bad about it," the bartender said, and turned away.

He lifted the shot glass toward his mouth, then lowered it and slowly turned his head to look at the bartender, who was filling a mug from the draught faucet. He waited until the bartender had filled three mugs for the Teamsters Union organizers. Then he called to the bartender, "What was that you said?"

The bartender didn't look at him. One of the middle-aged men was paying for the beer. The bartender rang up the sale, then came walking up behind the bar, still not looking at him. As the bartender walked past him, he reached across the bar and touched the white sleeve. The bartender stopped and said, not looking at him, "You better go home, mister."

"I want another drink."

Then the bartender looked at him. "No, you don't."

"Listen, Mike—"

"That's another thing, mister. My name ain't Mike to you. You call a man by his name only when you know him. And you don't know me. You don't know anybody here."

He said aloud to himself, "I knew her."

"No, you didn't," the bartender said. "You didn't know her at all. She was just like that drink in your glass, something you had a taste of now and then."

He looked at the bartender. The bartender was a

partially bald and chunkily built man with a former prize fighter's face, the nose battered, the lips thickened, one ear somewhat puffed and twisted. The bartender stood there waiting for him to say something and he tried to say something but it was impossible. He took a deep breath and went on looking at the bartender.

"I'm sorry I said that." The bartender spoke with his head lowered. "That was a crumby thing to say." Then suddenly and spasmodically he turned his head and shouted at the other customers, "What are you bastards staring at? Why don't you mind your own goddamn business?"

"We feel bad too," the little Spanish-looking man said with tears in his voice. "We all of us feel very bad about Lita."

"Poor child," the fat shapeless gray-haired woman said. "The poor, poor child."

"Aw, shut the hell up," the bartender shouted. "Whatcha think I'm running here, a funeral parlor?" He had his lips pressed hard against his teeth. His hand moved convulsively, going inside the white apron toward his trousers pocket. He pulled out some loose change and scattered it blindly along the surface of the bar, the silver coins rolling and skidding down toward the drinkers at the other end. "Let's have a polka or something, for Christ's sake. Somebody put a nickel in the goddamn jukebox."

The little Spanish-looking man selected a nickel from among the coins and went to the jukebox. For

some moments the room was quiet while the machine
lifted the record from its slot and lowered it into place.
Then the air of the taproom was shattered with hot
jumping jazz, the trumpets shrieking and the cymbals
clattering. One of the middle-aged men from the
Teamsters Union yelled, "That ain't no polka."

The little Spanish-looking man yelled, "Is Stanley
Kenton, he play good music."

The teamsters' representative banged his hand flat
on the bar and said, "I defy any music critic to tell me
that's music." He went on with it but Kenton played
louder and drowned him out.

The bartender poured a double shot for Bevan and
then poured one for himself. He made a waving gesture to indicate that this was on the house. They
touched glasses and drank and then the bartender
leaned across the bar and got his face close to Bevan's,
saying confidentially, "We got a new one, George. You
see her?"

"You mean the one in the booth? The blonde?"

"Yeah," the bartender said. "She ain't bad, either.
I've had her myself a coupla times and she really ain't
bad."

"Maybe I'll talk to her."

"Sure," the bartender said. "Go on over and talk
to her."

And say what? he asked himself. You came here to
talk to Lita. And Lita isn't here. Lita isn't anywhere.
That's an established fact and there's nothing you can
do about it. All right, let's say it's a damn shame and let

it go at that. But here we arrive at another established
fact. You can't drop it that easily. So I think what we
need here is another drink. Of course, our primary
need is a punch in the face from Mike's big right hand.
It would make us feel a lot better, and it would certainly reduce the guilt. Oh, Bevan, you heel, you louse,
you hypocrite, she's horizontal in a wooden box and
you're the engineer who put her there. Because you
handled her as if she were merchandise. It never
occurred to you that she was a living organism with
a mind and a soul and feelings. You want to start
remembering? Go on, then, remember the night she
said that in her book she rated you high. And in your
book you had her listed as a Tenth Avenue tramp,
strictly slum material that you couldn't take to dinner
at Longchamps, because she wouldn't blend with the
decor there. So what you did, you perfect gentleman
solid citizen lousy hypocrite, you came down from your
high-rent district to this low-rent hunting ground,
where you found it so easy and convenient to...

"Mike." He nearly choked on it. "Pour me another."

The bartender studied his eyes. "You all right?"

He nodded quickly, convulsively. "I'm doing great.
Hurry and pour me another."

The bartender shrugged and obeyed and went on
obeying for an hour, during which Bevan consumed
some fourteen double shots, not moving once from
that spot where he stood at the bar. But although
he was making a concerted effort to get drunk, the
lightweight cloud of drunkenness refused to come.

Instead it was on the order of an iron yoke pushing down on his shoulders, getting heavier with each drink, sending him deeper into the downward-slanting corridor where there were no lamps and very little air, where the only sound was a female voice that came from very far away. It said, "Don't leave me. Oh, please don't leave me." Of course, it was Lita saying now what she'd ached to say then when they'd had that farewell talk on the telephone. So now he replied soundlessly into the invisible mouthpiece. "What else can I do? What else can I do?" But she failed to provide an answer. And so quite naturally the only thing to do was to order another double shot and buy a round for the house.

Some twenty minutes later his bloodstream couldn't take it and he passed out. The bartender dragged him to an empty booth and he slept there until closing time. When the bartender woke him, he went into the lavatory and threw up. He came out grinning at the bartender and saying, "Where'd the blonde go? I wanna see the blonde."

"Can you make it home all right?"

"I want the blonde, that's what I want."

The bartender was helping him toward the street door. "Come on, you're O.K. I'll put you in a taxi."

"No blonde? Why can't I have the blonde?"

The bartender took a close look at him and saw he wasn't drunk. It was something else, something that had no connection with drunkenness.

He said, "I require that blonde. I tell you, I need

it, I need it something awful. You have no idea how much I need it." He was leaning heavily against the bartender's shoulder. "So why should I go home? What's the point in going home? There's nothing there, nothing I can use. You see what I mean? No, you don't see what I mean. All right, we'll try to make it clear. I'm looking for the blonde and I'm not referring to the blonde I have at home. The blonde I have at home is a very fine girl, really exceptional quality. Only trouble is, she's not a woman. That is, she's not a woman in the full sense of the word. Or the fundamental sense of the word, if you prefer to put it that way. So what this situation calls for is the blonde you wanted me to talk to."

"She went out a with a customer," the bartender said.

"She did?" He blinked a few times. "Why'd she do that? Why couldn't she wait for me?"

"She'll see you another time." The bartender patted his shoulder consolingly. "Tell you what. You come back tonight and—"

He shook his head slowly, then faster, then very fast, emphatically. "No," he said. "No, I won't come back tonight. Or any other night." He was looking up toward the ceiling, frowning thoughtfully and somewhat technically. And then, as though he were addressing an audience of solemn faces, "It strikes me, gentlemen, that we're dealing here with what appears to be a lost cause."

They were at the street door and the bartender

opened it. He smiled at the bartender and they shook hands and he walked out.

He kept his word and never went back to Hallihan's. From that day on he did his drinking in conservative, sedate establishments where unescorted women were not allowed. It didn't take long for the drinking to become a daytime as well as a nighttime habit, but he managed to handle it very nicely, managed to walk straight, his eyes steadily focused, holding his glass steadily, his voice always steady, so that no one could tell that his brain was drenched with alcohol. It took considerable effort to handle it that way, but he didn't mind. He almost enjoyed the straining effort it took, as though the strain of hiding the drunkenness were part of the price he had to pay for the drinking. And sometimes, when his stomach couldn't take it, and when his liver started raising hell, he enjoyed that too. He really liked the idea of paying the price.

He had the drinking habit and he had it good. Or bad, although he preferred to think it was good. Cora discovered it one day when he forgot to chew chlorophyll gum before entering the apartment. She asked him if he'd been drinking and he said yes. She asked if he was doing a lot of drinking and he said yes. Then he said he intended to keep on drinking and he hoped she wouldn't mind too much. He said he needed the drinking in the same way that a ball club needs a pinch hitter, and if she wanted him to explain that, he'd be glad to. But she didn't ask him to explain. After that, the only times she spoke about his drinking were when his

stomach couldn't take food, and then she'd lecture him
quietly and patiently, stating physiological facts she'd
read in newspaper health columns and magazines.

The drinking became bad when he reached the
point of trying to fight it. This happened after a partic-
ularly difficult night when Cora started one of her
health lectures and suddenly faltered in the middle of
it, breaking down and weeping, collapsing to her knees
at his feet and clutching his wrists, begging him to stop
drinking, at least to cut it down to a reasonable degree.
He promised he'd try. He began trying very hard to
keep the promise.

It was an extremely painful promise. The less he
drank, the worse he felt. And eventually it led him to
the neurologist, who couldn't do a thing about it
except to recommend a change of scenery.

Some change, he thought, sitting there in the chair
near the window. We're situated here in the Laurel
Rock Hotel in the city of Kingston on the island of
Jamaica. We're here in the British West Indies, some
sixteen hundred miles from Manhattan. But what it
amounts to is no change at all. It's the same gloomy
picture. It's the picture of yourself sliding downhill.

He got up from the chair and took another look
through the window. For only a moment he looked
down at the swimming pool, the gay colors of the
beach umbrellas and cabanas. After that he was
focusing past the wall that separated the Laurel Rock
from the crowded low-rent area where the Negroes
lived. As he gazed at the littered streets and shabby

hovels that were never displayed in the travel folders, he was thinking, Maybe that's where you belong.

His eyes narrowed cunningly. The corners of his mouth came up just a little to shape a thin conniving smile, as though he were building a practical joke to play on someone.

He said to himself, All right, let's try it. Let's put this lowlife in a place where he can feel at home.

The smile was fixed stiffly on his lips as he walked out of the room.

Chapter Three

He did considerable walking. It wasn't the casual strolling of a tourist taking in the sights. There was a certain purposefulness in his stride, as though he had something definite in mind, some special destination. The natives paid little or no attention to him. They got the impression that he was some city official or consulate employee headed somewhere on important business. Of course, if they'd known he was a tourist, they would have swarmed around him, trying to sell him souvenirs and postcards and whatnot, and those with nothing to sell would have begged him for a handout. In the slums of Kingston there are a great many street beggars and their ages range from five to eighty-five. They are very persistent, much more persistent than the countless women who sit in doorways displaying strings of beads and woven hats and baskets. But they are not so persistent as the taxi drivers. The taxi drivers of Kingston are famous for their persistence. They sell their transportation like carnival pitchmen who can't take no for an answer. It's mostly the tourists that keep them in business, and it's been said that they've developed a scent for tourists; they can smell one coming from several blocks away. This is no reflection on the tourists, although many natives are agreed that tourists in general have a smell all their own.

But this taxi driver didn't catch it with his nose. He caught it with his sharp eyes. Several hours ago he'd seen the neatly attired man walking past, had seen him again some ninety minutes ago, and now, seeing him for the third time, noticed that he walked more slowly, somewhat aimlessly.

The taxi driver was leaning against the battered fender of a very old Austin. As Bevan approached, the taxi driver moved and blocked his path and said, "Where you go, mon?"

"I wouldn't know," Bevan said, standing there and waiting for the Jamaican to step aside. "I wouldn't have the least idea."

The taxi driver said, "You looking for…"

"I don't know what I'm looking for," Bevan said, addressing the statement to no one in particular.

"Perhaps I can be of aid." The Jamaican's dark face was solemn.

"I doubt it," Bevan murmured, gazing past him. "I seriously doubt it."

"What hotel you stay at?"

Bevan looked at him. "For Christ's sake— Oh, all right, the Laurel Rock. So what?"

"Believe me, mon, you have a long walk. De distance is certainly not for walking. If you permit, I will drive you to de Laurel Rock."

"I can walk it," Bevan said vaguely. "I like to walk."

"Believe me, mon, dat is not de point. De point is"—the Jamaican aimed a forefinger at the darkening sky—"it is getting late."

Bevan smiled dimly. "You're right about that." The

way he said it, it had no connection with the hour of the day. His voice was almost inaudible as he said. "You're so right."

The Jamaican frowned slightly, detecting something odd in the man's tone, the man's eyes. But of course the important thing was the fare, and he went on with the sales talk. "Believe me, mon, dis vicinity is not safe for a tourist after dark. Many bandits and treacherous people about."

"Really bad?" Bevan smiled.

The taxi driver nodded solemnly. "Bad, mon."

"That's fine," Bevan said. "I'd like to meet them. I'm a rotten apple myself."

The taxi driver gave him a side glance. "Excuse me, mon. You are perhaps joking wid me?"

"I couldn't be more serious."

For some moments the Jamaican was quiet. He was wondering how to handle this problem. It was definitely a problem; he had the feeling he was dealing with something very much out of the ordinary.

Bevan was saying, "All right, Roscoe. Take me for a ride."

"To de Laurel Rock?"

"No," Bevan said. "Away from the Laurel Rock. As far away as I can get."

Without sound the Jamaican said, I think this one is crazy and the practical thing for me to do is leave him alone. I am never comfortable around crazy people.

"Tell you what," Bevan said. "Take me back to Hallihan's."

"Hallihan's?"

"It's only a short ride," Bevan said. His voice fell off and became a low groan. "It's at Fiftieth Street and Tenth Avenue."

The taxi driver played with that one for a moment, couldn't do anything with it, and finally said, "Do you know where you are? You are in Kingston, Jamaica."

"Correction." Bevan grinned at him. "I'm located exactly three miles south of nowhere."

The Jamaican decided he'd had enough. He stepped aside, walked quickly to the parked Austin, climbed in, and started the engine.

Bevan stood gazing at the little old car as it chugged away. The grin was fading from his lips and he was saying aloud, "Nobody cares." And then, with a shrug, "Well, why the hell should they?"

He glanced around, looking for any sign that offered drinks for sale.

There were no such signs in the immediate vicinity. He didn't know what street he was on. It was a quiet street and it was empty of people. He moved slowly through the stillness and the increasing darkness. There were no lamps along this street and gradually he developed a feeling of uneasiness mingled with the contented realization that this was the way it ought to be. It was a weird mixture of feelings, but of course he had no idea it was weird; he wasn't trying to study it or measure it while it hit him. It hit him lightly, almost caressingly.

Bevan turned a corner and found himself on Barry Street.

Barry is a somewhat narrow thoroughfare north of Harbour and south of Queen. These are wider streets, better paved, appearing rather prominently on the city map. Harbour Street has many retail shops in addition to warehouses and brokerage establishments, and Queen is more or less the main drag, very noisy and somewhat frolicsome at night, brightly lit with its native hotels and saloons and eateries. In comparison, Barry Street is not much more than a hungry-looking alley. The fact remains, however, that more money changes hands along Barry. It is a distribution center for a special type of commerce that can't be advertised on the printed page or billboards.

The late-night action along Barry Street takes place mostly in the back rooms. The majority of the customers are merchant seamen off the vessels docked in Kingston Harbor. In the dismal gray hours of early morning they come away from Barry Street with bloodshot eyes, breathing air that tastes like grease mixed with vinegar. And later, in waterfront bars throughout the globe, they advise their seagoing drinking companions, "If you ever hit Kingston, Jamaica, stay the hell away from Barry Street."

"Bad?"

"Worse than bad. You're bound to get clipped, and you're lucky if you get out of it alive."

But negative publicity has a magnetic effect on most merchant seamen. It amounts to a dare, and as a group they enjoy biting at dares. And so they are lured to Barry Street, and they enter its dark stillness with chips on their shoulders, moving along with a swagger that says, Not this one, mate. This one'll come out ahead of the game.

And some of them do. But most of them don't. Most of them come out with empty pockets and bleeding mouths and battered heads. Many of them come out with their hands pressed tightly against their knife-slashed ribs and bellies. And the very next time their boat docks in Kingston, they head directly for Barry Street.

They enter the shabby splintered doorways under hand-printed signs that read, "Licensed to sell alcoholic beverages." So in the front rooms everything is legitimate and they purchase the rum at the standard rate, sixpence or a dime for the water glass half filled. This bargain price puts considerable liquor down their throats and eventually nudges them toward the back rooms, where there is gambling or girls or perhaps nothing more than someone holding a blackjack and waiting patiently. The windup is that they're either cheated at cards or robbed by the girls or slugged senseless. And whether they know it or not, they look for this to happen. If it doesn't happen, they keep forcing the issue, trying to make it happen. There is a metaphysical reason that seamen in general behave this way, and it is not too difficult to probe. The oceans were made for fishes, not for two-legged creatures. So the effect of long weeks or months aboard the slow-moving freighters is like the slow burning of a fuse attached to a firecracker.

On this night four Norwegian seamen walked into

Winnie's Place on Barry Street. They came in quietly
and remained quiet while they took a table. Winnie
gave them a quick once-over from where she stood
behind the bar, and she knew they wouldn't be quiet
for long.

She sighed inwardly. She had a headache and she
was suffering from a chest cold. All day long she'd
been hoping there wouldn't be any excitement tonight.
Not that she especially minded the excitement; it was
the thought of cleaning up afterward that bothered her.

She was a middle-aged spinster who had worked
hard all her life and hadn't had much fun. Her deal-
ings with men were on the dreary side, and although
she wanted to like them, they didn't give her many
openings. It was probably because of her looks. Her
muscatel-colored skin was badly blemished from
smallpox in childhood, and she didn't have much of a
chin. Another factor that kept her unmarried and
more or less untouched was her curveless build. She
was decidedly flat-fronted and flat-backed. It amounted
to five feet seven and 160 pounds of rather unattrac-
tive female.

But it didn't bother her too much. A long time ago
she'd made up her mind she wouldn't allow it to
bother her. The only thing that really bothered her
was this business of cleaning up after the turmoil of
smashing bottles and breaking chairs and getting
phlegm and blood all over the floor. She took another
look at the four Norwegians and wondered how long it
would be before they started something.

In addition to the Norwegians, there were perhaps

a dozen customers in the place. Three of them were Chinese cooks off a boat from Australia, and all the others were natives except for Bevan, who sat on a stool beside the window with his glass of rum on the windowsill. When he'd first come in, they'd looked at him curiously. But now he'd been here for hours and they'd got tired of wondering who he was and what he wanted in this place. They'd gradually arrived at the conclusion that whoever he was, the only thing he was after was alcohol and a lot of it.

The Norwegians remained quiet for perhaps a quarter of an hour. Then one of them got up and came toward Winnie and said in English, "Where is the music?"

"No music," Winnie said. "De piccolo is broken."

"What piccolo? Who performs on this piccolo?"

"De music machine," Winnie said. "We call it de piccolo," she explained. "It necessitates repairs and dey take it to de factory."

The Norwegian considered this for a few moments, came close to accepting it, then shook his head decisively and said loudly, "For sure, that is no excuse."

Winnie didn't say anything. She aimed her attention past the Norwegian, focusing on the three Chinese, who were saying with their fingers that they wanted more Red Stripe. Turning away from the Norwegian, Winnie opened the ice cabinet and was taking out three bottles of beer when he reached across the bar and put a grip on her arm. He did it quickly and it jolted her. She dropped two bottles but caught the third as it fell, her free hand holding it tightly around the neck, her free arm rigid at her side as she heard the Norwegian saying, "For sure, when I make the talk to someone, I demand the respect of being heard."

He tightened his grip on her arm. She stood there showing him her profile, her other arm now loose at her side. But her fingers were firm around the neck of the Red Stripe bottle.

"And also," the Norwegian said, "when I make the talk to someone, for sure he should look at me."

Winnie didn't move. She was waiting for him to let go of her arm. He was a thickset man with very thick, strong fingers. His thumb was pressing into the vein at her elbow and it was hurting her.

"You show me half your face," the Norwegian said. "For sure, I want to see all your face when I make the talk to you."

She wanted very much to hit him with the bottle. She wasn't the least bit angry. Actually, she felt sorry for him. His voice told her he was terrible unhappy and homesick. Besides, he was rather young, and she always had pity for the young ones far away from their homeland. But if she didn't hit him, someone else would do it, and that would start a fracas. She was wondering technically what she could do to prevent a fracas. His thumb was pushing harder into her elbow and she decided the feasible thing to do was give in. She turned and showed him her full face and said, "Very well, mon. I listen to you."

"Good," the Norwegian said. He gave an approving nod, his blue-gray eyes very cold and authoritative. "For sure, all I ask for is a reasonable quantity of politeness."

But he was somewhat taken away with it. He was forgetting to let go of her arm.

One of the Jamaicans came forward and stood beside the Norwegian and said to him, "You are not so polite yourself."

Without looking at the Jamaican, the Norwegian said, "Get away from me, black man."

"What is that?" the Jamaican asked quietly, "What did you call me?"

Before the Norwegian could answer, one of his shipmates was up from the table and moving in quickly, saying to him in the language of their country, "You are behaving badly."

"Keep out of this," he said in their language.

"You are behaving like an imbecile," the other Norwegian said. He looked at the Jamaican, then at Winnie, trying to tell them with his eyes that he was ashamed of his compatriot's conduct.

The thickset Norwegian released Winnie's arm. He turned slowly and faced his shipmate and said, "Now you have done something. For sure, you have hurt my feelings."

"And what is the remedy for that?"

"I am not completely certain. I am trying to decide."

The two Norwegians at the table were getting up and coming toward them. And then it was getting rather crowded at the bar as several of the Jamaicans came forward. Winnie was still holding the bottle of Red Stripe at her side. She was saying, "All right, everybody. Now you go back to de tables. It is finished."

"What is finished?" the thickset Norwegian asked.

"I say it is finished," Winnie said. She spoke more loudly. She raised her arm to display the bottle in her hand. "I am chairman of dis conference and I say it is finished."

"For sure, it is not finished," the thickset Norwegian said. "It cannot be finished because it has not yet commenced."

"That is a logical statement," a Jamaican said. "I think that is very logical."

"You really think so, black man?" The thickset seaman smiled. It was a leering smile, and as it came sliding off his face the other Norwegian punched him very hard in the mouth. He fell back against the Jamaican whom he had previously antagonized. The Jamaican aimed a punch at his head and missed and caught one of the other Norwegians between the eyes. So then it was started and Winnie saw a Jamaican pulling a knife from somewhere inside his shirt, and she swung the bottle in a sideward arc that ended alongside his face, the bottle breaking against his cheekbone. He dropped the knife as he went down with slivers of glass planted deep in his cheek, with the blood coming out very fast and gushing over his screeching mouth. One of the seamen leaned over to pick up the knife and a Jamaican snatched a bottle of Red Stripe lager off the bar and broke it over his head. Then some of them were scrambling to get at the knife and some were reaching for bottles on the shelf behind the bar. Among the Jamaicans certain personal animosities came to the surface and some were using their fists on each other. The thickset Norwegian was slugging head to head with the Norwegian who had called him an imbecile. While all this was happening, the three Chinese cooks were trying to make their way toward a side door that led to the alley. One of them managed to make it, and the others were blocked by the entangled combatants, some of them rolling on the floor, some of them sailing back from the impact of fists or elbows, all of them gasping and sobbing and grunting hard with the frenzied need to hit something, anything.

On the other side of the room, Bevan had his head resting on the windowsill, his eyes half open and getting a rum-blurred close-up view of his empty glass. He heard the thudding, the banging and crashing and hammering, but the noises meant nothing to him. He was concentrating on the empty glass. It shouldn't be empty, he was thinking. It should have some rum in it.

He raised his head just a little and mumbled, "We're ready for another."

At that moment a Jamaican was hurling a chair at another Jamaican who had owed him four shillings for several weeks and had shown no inclination to pay. The chair came sailing at the man's head and he side-stepped gracefully. The chair continued on its way, missed Bevan's skull by a few inches, and went crashing through the window. Bevan blinked several times and said, "I didn't ask for that. I asked for a drink."

A moment later one of the Norwegians received a wallop in the face and it knocked him clear across the room. He collided with Bevan, who fell off the stool and sat down hard on the floor. The Norwegian was up instantly, taking a deep sobbing breath and returning to the skirmish. Bevan remained sitting on the floor, his shirt and tie and mohair suit now stained with blood from the Norwegian's mouth and nose. He looked down at his bloodstained clothes and shook his head with solemn disapproval.

"This won't do," he murmured. "This certainly calls for another drink."

He sat there waiting for someone to serve him a glass of rum.

On the other side of the room the free-for-all was gaining momentum. It had passed the phase of rum-induced fury; now it was blood-induced. The more blood they spilled, the more they wanted to spill.

Winnie had decided there was nothing she could do except seek a safety zone. Now she was half crouched behind the bar, expecting its wooden sides to crumble at any moment. Already some of the boards had given way. The weakened, splintered bar was creaking and groaning as their lunging, tumbling, staggering bodies came against it. Winnie was estimating how much it would cost to put up a new bar, or anyway hire a carpenter to fix this one. She felt somewhat victimized, and her lower lip came out sullenly.

She thought, there's no way to sue for damages. That's one of the disadvantages of this business. What you ought to do, Winnie, is get out of this business. And do what? Go to work in some factory? Or in the fields? Or sit in a stall in the marketplace selling mangoes and limes? With your face wet with tears at

the end of the day when you look at the fruit and vegetables unsold and there's no consolation whatsoever,
not even the sight of other tearful faces? No, you don't
want that. You had a taste of it once, the tobacco
factory and the sugar fields and the marketplace, and
you concluded that's for the fools, the soft ones, the
timid ones. And yet, Winnie, you're a fool yourself, all
things considered. You try to treat them nice and look
what they do to your place. Just look at what they do to
this decent establishment that you sweat and strain to
keep clean, the glasses always washed and no dust on
the tables, no roaches on the floor. Yes, I insist this is
a decent establishment, not like the other houses
on Barry Street, with the dirty goings-on in the back
rooms. In the back rooms of this house there are no
girls, no gambling, no hired rough man waiting there
with something heavy in his hand. But what are the
dividends from your honesty? And how do they show
their appreciation? Look at you now. You're hiding
here like a lonely frightened mouse, and if you raise
your head another inch it might get fractured.

    She went on pouting about it, remaining crouched
behind the bar. A bleeding Jamaican came flying over
the top and landed in a senseless heap beside her. As
he went deeper into slumber, he used her head for a
pillow. Without giving any thought to it, she put her
arm around him, sort of cradling him. That made it
less lonely here, even though there was still no one to
talk to.

    Some moments later one of the Norwegians de-
scribed an awkward somersault that brought him

down behind the bar. He came to rest on the other side of Winnie, with his feet sticking up in the air. She gave him a push that put him right side up, and then, semiconscious, he fell against her. So that now she didn't feel lonely at all, and the sullen dismal pouting was gone. She sat there between the slumbering Jamaican and the dazed Norwegian, her arms around their shoulders. There was a dim, wistful smile on her lips, sort of a Madonna smile. Her flat, dried-up breasts seemed to be filling; she sensed the flow, the slow serene current of feeling that they really needed her now.

It was a very pleasant feeling and she drifted deeper into it, became lost in it, and didn't hear the noises of battle that came crashing in from the other side of the bar. She didn't even hear the customer who was pounding on the bar and demanding another drink.

"Come on, I'm thirsty," Bevan complained. He hit his clenched hands against the wooden surface of the bar. "What's the matter here? The bartenders on strike?"

He'd given up waiting for a waitress and had managed to get to his feet, had worked his way slowly and staggeringly across the room, moving through the chaos of all-out combat that enveloped him and slammed into him but somehow failed to knock him off his feet. He was dimly aware that something hectic was happening, but it didn't mean anything to his liquor-soaked brain. He wanted another drink and that was all.

Again he rapped his knuckles against the top of the

bar. He said, "What's holding up the play? You think I'm a—" A fist meant for someone else's face clipped him on the side of the head. He staggered and almost fell, his hands clutching at the edge of the bar. He blinked a few times, then tried again. "You think I'm a loafer or something? You think—" And then from the other side he was bumped violently by a Jamaican sailing backward after taking a hard punch in the mouth. In almost the same instant someone's elbow caught him in the ribs, and a broken chair leg aimed at someone's skull hit Bevan's shoulder instead. He gave a sigh of weary annoyance and said, "Oh, leave me alone, for Christ's sake. Go play in the yard or something." Then, resuming his attempt to purchase a drink, "Let's examine the facts of this matter. I said I'm not a loafer. You hear me? I'm not here to take up space. I'm a cash customer. I'll prove it." His hand groped for his lapel, missed it a few times, then found it, found the inside breast pocket, and took out the wallet. He opened the wallet, displaying green paper and saying indignantly, "There. You see? You see?"

But it didn't get him a drink. It didn't even get a spoken reply. He sighed again, closed the wallet, and put it back in his pocket. "O.K.," he said, more sadly than indignantly. "If that's the way it is, I'll take my trade somewhere else."

He meant it, too. He seriously meant it. He had to get that drink, and the need for it throbbed in his brain as he gazed around, searching for the nearest exit. He saw the side door at the far end of the bar and started pushing his way toward it, slowly forcing a path through the swarming, seething mass of wild-eyed men. Somehow they had him listed as a neutral, and without giving any thought to it they refrained from banging at him as he made his way toward the side door.

But there was one Jamaican whose attention had been drawn to the displayed wallet and the thick sheaf of green bills it contained. The Jamaican's eyes became narrow and calculating. He detached himself from the whirlpool of battle and his expression was catlike as he followed the drunken tourist toward the exit that led to a dark alley.

Bevan arrived at the door and opened it and stumbled outside. The alley was very dark. It was littered with garbage and tin cans and empty bottles. He stood there blinking and frowning, trying to get his bearings. The thing to do was make it back to Barry Street and find another house where they'd sell him a drink. He mumbled aloud, "Which way is Barry Street?" and then decided it must be that faint glow of lamplight filtering through the darkness not very far away. He took a few steps in that direction, tripped over a garbage can, and fell flat. He pulled himself up, stepped past the overturned garbage can, then kicked aside some empty bottles, saying to anyone who cared to listen, "Where's the street cleaners around here? Why don't they get to work?"

The reply was a footstep that he didn't hear, and a moment later it was a blackjack coming toward his skull. But he was a poor target, swaying drunkenly, and the blackjack only grazed his shoulder. He thought it was some night bird flying past, and turned his head to see if another night bird was coming. The lamplight drifting in from Barry Street showed him the black shape of a leather-covered cudgel, above it the black face of the Jamaican. He shrugged and then said, "Come on, take me to a bar. We'll get a drink."

The Jamaican worked the blackjack in a sideward arc aimed at Bevan's temple. Bevan's arm came up instinctively and he took the impact just below his elbow. The Jamaican became impatient and made another try. Again Bevan took it on his forearm, the force of it going through his arm and against his ribs and sending him sideways going down. He landed on his hip, looked up and saw the Jamaican's eyes telling him this was for real, and told himself he had to do something, he couldn't just sit there and take it.

As the blackjack came down again, he rolled away, then rolled back so that his weight came in hard against the Jamaican's legs. The Jamaican went down but came up fast, still holding onto the blackjack. Bevan glanced around, saw an empty bottle nearby, reached out, and grabbed it. In that instant the Jamaican was closing in and swinging the blackjack. Bevan raised the bottle, using it for a shield. The blackjack hit the bottle, cracking it along the side near the bottom. In Bevan's hand the broken bottle gleamed with a sudden importance that caused the Jamaican to hesitate. But he came lunging in again, his right hand swinging the cudgel and his left hand shooting out to get inside Bevan's jacket. He was trying to do two things at once and it fouled him up;

the blackjack missed and his left hand swept past Bevan's shoulder. The impetus of his lunge ended his life. The cutting edge of the broken bottle sliced his throat and split his jugular vein. All he could do was make a few gurgling sounds, and then he was finished.

Bevan lifted himself to his feet. He looked down at the motionless body. It was resting face down. He said, "You all right?" For some moments he stood there waiting for an answer. Then somehow he knew there'd be no answer. But even so, he told himself, you'd better have a look and make sure. He leaned over and turned the body on its back. And then he was staring at the bulging unblinking eyes that started back at him and said, Look what you did. Look what you did to me.

He moved away from the corpse, headed blindly toward any place at all that would get him far away from here. He went down the alley away from Barry Street, through another alley, and then another. And finally he found himself on Harbour Street. In the distance he could see the lighted windows of the Laurel Rock Hotel.

Chapter Four

There was a side entrance that brought him into a foyer off the main lobby. At this late hour there was no doorman, no bellhops or attendants moving around. That helps some, he thought, looking down at his bloodstained clothes. His clothes were brightly, stickily stained with Norwegian and Jamaican blood.

The foyer had its own stairway. His rum-glazed eyes tried to focus on the stairs as he went up very slowly, somewhat zigzag. Some years ago he'd done some mountain climbing, and this was like a fifth-grade ascent; it seemed almost vertical, really a tricky proposition. He seriously wondered if he could make it to the third floor.

It took him several minutes to get to the third floor. He weaved and staggered along the corridor, arrived at 307, and began groping for the room key in whatever pocket he'd put it in. But somehow his fingers couldn't get anywhere near the right pocket. Finally he gave it up. He leaned his forehead against the door, hitting the heel of his palm against the wooden panel. It made only a small sound and he tried to hit the door harder but his arm lacked the power. His arm and all the rest of him felt like a lump of damp clay.

He went on hitting the door. Eventually he heard her calling, "Who is it?"

"The milkman," he said, wondering why he had to

put it that way. Or maybe it was better to put it that way.

"James?"

"Check," he said. His eyes were half closed and he was trying to grin. If she saw him grinning it might be easier for her. He wanted to make it easier for her. He said, "It's James the milkman."

The door opened. He was doing his best not to fall headlong into the room. He went on grinning as he swayed like a thin-stemmed plant in a stiff wind.

He couldn't see her yet. All he saw was something wispy white, sort of yellow on top. That's probably her hair, he thought, her adorable pale-gold tresses.

Cora pulled him into the room and closed the door. "Good evening," he said, and she said, "Just stand there. Don't touch anything." He heard her moving away, and then in the darkness she was at the windows, pulling the blinds down all the way.

"What's all the commotion?" he wanted to know. She didn't answer. She came toward him and went past him, going to the wall and flicking the light switch.

The ceiling bulbs were very bright and the light hurt his eyes. He stood there blinking hard. "The better to see me, my dear? What's there to see?"

"Can you walk?"

"Not hardly. I'll just float. Where do you want me to float?"

"Float into the bathroom."

"Why the bathroom? I'm not sick."

"I want you to take off your clothes," she said. "If

you take them off in here, you'll mess up the entire room."

"I guess you have a point there." But he didn't move. He was still grinning and blinking hard in the brightness of the room.

"Please go into the bathroom."

He didn't move. He put his fingers against his bloodstained jacket. "It's so sticky," he said. "It's like raspberry jam."

She said very slowly, "Will you please go into the bathroom?"

He went into the bathroom. He sat down on the tile floor. He bent over and tried to take off his shoes. Boola-boola, he sang without sound. And then, with sound, "Bulldog! Bulldog! Rah-rah-rah! E-li Yale!" His fingers fell away from the shoelaces and he toppled over at an acute angle that sent his head banging against the side of the bathtub. The impact, added to the rum and everything else, was just a little too much for him, and he went out.

Then hours later he opened his eyes. He saw thin streams of daylight seeping in through the blinds. Of course, the first thing he wanted was a drink. He reached mechanically for the phone on the table beside his bed. But then he saw her in the other bed. She was awake and she was looking at him.

"Oh, hello," he said.

She nodded toward the telephone. "What are you doing?"

"I thought I'd ring for a drink."

"Go ahead," she said. "Go right ahead."

"What's the matter?" And then, a trifle louder, "What's the matter with you?"

She didn't answer.

"All right, then," he said. "I'll ring for breakfast instead. What would you like for breakfast?"

"I don't want any breakfast."

He removed his hand from the telephone. "You know something? We haven't sampled much of their food. Keeps up like this, they'll think we're staging a hunger strike."

She was quiet for some moments. Then, not looking at him, "Why don't you go back to sleep? It's still rather early." She gestured toward the clock on the dresser. The hands pointed to a little after six-fifteen.

He looked at the face of the clock. He said, "Yes, it's very early. It's certainly too early in the morning to talk. Or let's change that. Let's say it's too late to talk. That is, unless you feel like talking."

"I wish you'd go back to sleep."

"All right, dear. Anything you say. You want me to sleep, I'll sleep. You want me not to wake up, I won't wake up."

"Is that necessary? Talking that way?"

He didn't reply. He was giving some serious thought to that question. But reaching for an answer was like groping in a dark deep pool, too dark and too deep. He said to himself, Let it alone, let it drift away. He said to Cora, "I hope you'll pardon me. I'm a trifle hazy this fine morning. Purely a matter of biochemistry, the natural effect of hundred-proof nectar of the sugar cane on John W. Hemoglobin, resulting in a rather unique color scheme, the red and white playing second fiddle to amber-colored corpuscles. Incidentally, how in God's name did I get in this bed?"

"I put you there."

"You did?" And then seriously, really meaning it, "Oh, I'm sorry about that. It must have been quite a strain."

She smiled at him. "You're not very heavy, James. And besides, I've done it before. I've done it so many times before."

"You sure have," he said. "You're a true friend and a boon companion and—"

"I put your clothes in the bathtub," she interrupted quietly. "I'm letting them soak, but of course it won't do any good, the suit is ruined. It's a pity, you wore it only a few times."

"Maybe if I have it dry-cleaned—"

"You can't do that," she said. "You know you can't do that."

He glanced around the room. "I wish this layout had a fireplace."

"Oh, well, we won't worry about it now. We'll think of something." But as she said it, her voice quivered.

The quivering came at him in a series of tiny waves that felt ice-cold, and he almost shivered as it went into him, telling him what an effort she was making to remain calm, her throat choked with the stifled questions: What happened last night? How did you get all that blood on your clothes? What are you trying to hide from me?

He gave a little sigh and said, "No use keeping you

guessing. You're due to find out sooner or later and it might as well come from me. What happened was"— and he was trying to shrug as he let it out—"a man tried to get my wallet."

"You didn't—"

"Yes, I did." He sighed again. "All he wanted was my money. I could have given him the money and let it go at that. Or let him hit me with the blackjack. He wouldn't have done much damage—he wasn't swinging for the fences. Just an infield single."

"James—"

"A broken bottle, that's what did it. I picked up the bottle and— Poor devil, he looked so full of life just before it happened."

"Maybe it didn't happen. After all, you were very drunk. You can't be sure—"

"I'm sure. I'm quite sure."

Then he looked at her. He saw she was sitting on the edge of her bed. Now her eyes were closed and she had her hands pressed against her chest. She seemed awfully frail and helpless sitting there, like a maiden captured by demons and about to be sacrificed. Or make it one demon, he thought. Just one. A rum-drunk demon, and when it wasn't rum it was gin and when it wasn't gin it was bourbon or rye or whatever they had to sell. Well, you've done it now. You've really given it to her this time. You've given it to her good and proper, mister. Strictly according to the rulebook used by your brother demons. We're all of us a very select group and we can't do it any other way; a chartered society of wasted protoplasm, each of us wearing the lodge pin with the one-word motto inscribed: Impotent.

So if we can't do it one way, we do it another. Some of us go to private showings of contraband cinema. And some go in for live showings where the admission is fifteen dollars and up. But that's too unsanitary for most of us. Most of us try very hard to be sanitary, or call it gentlemanly, call it anything you like, it's nevertheless a sham, a falsity. So it's always Halloween in this league; there isn't a single maneuver that's genuine. On the surface you cut his throat in self-defense, and under the surface, under all the rum and the silliness, your mood was homicidal. Now go ahead and try to deny that.

Try to deny you didn't mean to do it, you didn't want to do it. But remember, you can't be cagey with this party. This party knows you, sees inside you. All you can say to this party is: I saw something yesterday that set me off, started me on a campaign aimed at destruction. Yes, I looked out that window and saw her down there at the side of the swimming pool with the suddenly acquired boyfriend we've named Flatnose or Carrot-top or any name at all that tries to make it comical. But of course it wasn't comical, and when you walked out of the hotel and headed for God-knows-what, it was actually you-know-what and you won't admit it. Because you were completely disorganized, you lacked whatever it took to go down there to the swimming pool and confront them and assert your claim to this woman, assert your manhood.

Some manhood. The only thing you had was yellow

jelly inside that got to boiling up and boiling over and you felt the need to strike at something, destroy something.

That makes it premeditated, I guess. What do you mean, you guess? The taxi driver wasn't guessing when he took off in nothing flat. He saw it in your eyes and he knew his only move was rapid transfer. Oh, well, you must have thought without knowing you thought it: I missed getting this one but I'll get the next one.

At any rate, the windup came according to the blueprint. And who's the architect? He's an unseen instigator who specializes in the unpredictable. In this case he drew up a set of plans that started with two people sitting in beach chairs near a swimming pool, and ended with broken glass in the throat of a man I'd never seen before.

I think it would be entirely in order if you said all this out loud so she could know just what you are, what you're made of. But that's the tickler; it's this yellow jelly you're made of that causes the traffic jam and prevents a verbal statement. It would be interesting, though. It would be an interesting experiment if you could get all this past your lips.

He heard her saying, "—if you'd tell me about it."

"Sure," he said. "Sure, I'll tell you."

But he couldn't go on from there. He blinked several times, and gradually a vague grin drifted onto his lips. It was a hopeless and somewhat silly sort of grin. He let it stay there.

"Please," she said. "It's very important that you tell me."

The grin went away. He nodded in solemn agreement. And then he started to tell her. It was surprisingly easy to remember the events of last night and his account was complete and accurate. "So I walked out of Winnie's place through a side door and there was an alley. I didn't see him coming at me. He made a few tries with a blackjack and I picked up an empty bottle. The bottle got cracked and then I was on the ground and he was trying again with the blackjack. He had his other hand reaching toward my inside pocket where I keep my wallet. It must have been just then that I jabbed the bottle and the broken edge went into his throat."

Again she closed her eyes. She gave a shudder.

"I'm sorry," he murmured, "but you said I should tell you."

"Yes, of course." Then her eyes were open and she took a deep breath. She frowned somewhat technically and said, "Did anyone see?"

"I don't know. I don't think so."

She went on frowning. After some moments she said, "I think it'll be all right." And then the frown faded and she was smiling at him. "There's really nothing to worry about."

"I'm not worried," he said. He tried to return the smile. But his expression was more of a sickly grimace.

She studied his face. She said, "Please try to forget about it."

"Sure," he said. "I'll start right now. I'm checking it off"—he snapped his fingers—"just like that."

But it was no good. The sickly grimace stayed there.

"Now listen," she said. "According to what you've told me, you did it in self-defense. The man was trying to take your money and you had every right to protect yourself. There's certainly no reason to be so upset."

"You're right. You're absolutely right."

"The man was a criminal and he took his chance and lost. That's the only way to look at it."

He nodded again. But the twisted expression wouldn't leave his face.

She said, "Later today I'll take the clothes out of the bathtub and find some way to get rid of them. It shouldn't be much of a problem. I'll put them in a bag or something and throw them in the incinerator."

"No," he said, "I'll handle that."

"Please, James. Let me."

"You mean I'm liable to mess things up?"

"I didn't say—"

"You mean I'll get drunk again and make all sorts of mistakes and ruin everything. Isn't that what you mean?"

"Well—"

"Come on, say what you're thinking." He said it softly, almost amiably. "It makes it easier when you tell me what you're thinking."

She wasn't looking at him. "I'm thinking you look so tired and worn out—"

"And you feel sorry for me—"

"You're a nice person, James. You're very nice, really."

"Ha-ha. That's a nifty."

"If you'd only—"

"If I'd only change," he sang out, as though he were crooning into a microphone. "If I'd only stop the drinking, the ever dismal thinking, tra-la, tra-la, but it's such a hard task that you ask—of me, tra-la. And—"

"James—"

"And so," he went on singing, his voice very much off key, "there isn't a chance to recapture romance—"

"Stop it."

"You're worse off than a nance, you can't get hot pants." He was pointing accusingly at himself. "You—"

"Stop it! Stop it!"

"O.K." He smiled at her. He blew her a kiss. Then he rolled over face down on the pillow. In a few moments he was floating downward into sleep.

It was fitful slumber. The rhythm of it was distorted, and instead of total blackout it was more like flashes of gray bouncing off a black screen. Although his limbs were motionless, his brain hopped around in circles trying to get away from big billboards. All the billboards read the same, and it wasn't an advertisement, it was a public announcement. It stated: "This man destroyed a human being and it wasn't an accident, and don't believe him when he claims self-defense. He's a dyed-in-the-wool slayer if there ever was one. He went out to spill some blood and he spilled it, that's all. Can we let him get away with that?"

"No," he mumbled in his sleep. "Certainly not."

Cora heard it. She opened her eyes and looked toward his bed. Now he was resting on his side, and she could see his face all tightened up in the sickly grimace. It was as though he wore a mask and were trying to scare her away.

And maybe that's what I should do, she thought. Get away from him. Get out of this bed and get dressed and go away, far away. Because now it's really catastrophe. It's like the earth quaking and falling apart, the walls of your house collapsing, and if you don't get away you'll be crushed. Look at him, he's crushed already. He's a wreck, that's what he is. What you see there is wreckage.

Yes, I think he's just about hit bottom. I think he's reached the point of total ruin and there's nothing you can do for him now.

Do you pity him? she asked herself. No, you don't pity him. He did it to himself. He brought it on by slow degrees and then faster degrees and finally it blew up in his face and knocked him for a loop. For many loops. For endless loops. To send him sailing far away to some dizzy, goofy place where every day is Halloween. Just look at him. He seems actually pleased. He's saying he likes it there, he took the road going there and now he's there and it's very nice, he likes it. So you know there's no reason to pity him.

What I'll do is, I'll leave him. Yes, that's what I'll do. You will? Of course. I will. What else can I do? Can I let it go on like this? I've had enough of it, too much of it. I just can't take any more of it.

Take more of what? You'll need to pin it down before you try an answer. I think the answer is you're taking only what you're dishing out. You've been dishing it out for years and years, all the nine years of living with him and putting him through hell. A hell where it's all ice instead of fire, a frozen hell where he tried and tried to bring warmth but you wouldn't respond because you couldn't respond. He reached out for you and you were cold. He held you in his arms and you shivered. Without sound you said to him, Don't—please don't. So finally it was like getting an idea across to him and he stopped trying.

I think you'd better stop trying. I mean stop trying to make excuses for him. Let's face it, girl. You know he's on the weak side, very much on the weak side. If he weren't weak-kneed and weak-brained he wouldn't need all that alcohol. But he needs it, he can't do without it, and that puts him down there with all the other weaklings, the lushes, the unfunny buffoons who are always getting into scraps, who are always adding difficulty onto difficulty. Yes, he's down there in that category, and you can't lift him up. There's nothing to work with; there's only that warped, silly grin on his face.

If only he were more of a man...

I mean, if only he were more on the order of what's-his-name.

What's his name? Why can't I remember? He sat there in the beach chair talking about Ibsen while all the time I couldn't concentrate on Ibsen because I was looking at what he was showing me. He was showing me his bulging muscles and his rock-hard stomach and his hairy chest. I wish he were here now.

What's that again?

What do you mean, you wish he were here now?

You can't mean that. If he ever tried to touch you, you'd freeze. And maybe scream for help. His hands are so large, the fingers so thick, and there's so much strength there and you're so afraid of him, so terribly afraid that he'll try to put his hands on you, he'll try to—

It mustn't happen, she said to herself. I mustn't give it a chance to happen. If he tries to talk to me, I'll brush him off politely, that's what I'll do. You mean, you'll try. The way you're trying now to tell yourself it mustn't happen but you want it to happen but it mustn't happen, it's so filthy and shameful and horrible to think about and will you please remember what Mother said? She said, "Don't get yourself dirty." Come to think of it, I feel like taking a bath. Yes, it's so hot in here, it's so awfully hot and sticky, I guess it's close to a hundred out there. This bed is like an oven and you're just like butter getting greasy in the frying pan. But I'll tell you something, it isn't a matter of the weather out there. Can we understand that? Yes, let's understand that. And please, let's get up and get out of this bed and take a bath.

Chapter Five

It was noon when she woke him up. He saw she was dressed. She looked as though she'd been up and about for hours. He asked her what she'd been doing. She said she'd had breakfast, and then she'd written some letters and postcards. Also, she'd got rid of his bloodstained clothes. She mentioned that offhandedly, as though the stains were fruit juice or ink, rather than blood. She wasn't looking at him as she said it, and he made no comment.

They went downstairs together. They walked into the dining room. Nearly all of the tables were empty. Lunch had not yet been announced and there were just a few late breakfasters. A waiter came over with a menu. Bevan was very hungry and he ordered figs in cream, scrambled eggs and kidneys, toasted muffins, and a pot of coffee. As the waiter moved away, Cora said, "I'm so glad you're eating something. It'll do you good."

He smiled at her. "You'll have coffee with me?"

"All right."

"They have good coffee here."

"Yes, it's very good."

"It's so much better than instant coffee."

"I'll make a note of that." She smiled at him. "When we get home, I'll buy a percolator."

"They'll think you're old-fashioned," he said. "Percolators went out a long time ago."

"Not really. They still sell percolators."

"But not like they used to. Now it's instant coffee. The trend is toward speed. It's all instant this and instant that, and quick freezing and so forth. We're all in such a hurry."

She nodded. "That's so true." She was gazing past him. "We'd be so much better off if we took our time, wouldn't we?"

"That depends," he said.

"Depends on what?"

"On how much time we have."

"You mean these bombs they're inventing?"

"I guess that's part of it. But I wasn't referring to that. It's more a matter of individual cases. Some people are older at the age of two than they are at eighty-two."

She looked at him. "How is that?"

"The two-year-old might never reach his third birthday. But Grandpa might live to be ninety."

She mixed a frown with a smile. "I never thought of it that way."

"Neither did I. Not until recently. Not until just now, as a matter of fact."

"What made you think of it?" Her head had turned slightly, and she was giving him a sideways look.

He was quiet for some moments. And then, as he lit a cigarette, "I don't know, it just hit me. Maybe these ideas float around in the air until someone gets in the way and gets hit."

She tapped her finger against her chin. "If that's the case, anyone at all has a chance to make history."

"Yes, I guess that's what it amounts to. Only thing is, before you can come out with something new, you've got to take it in. Or rather, you've got to be in a position to accept it. Like what they say about the apple falling off the tree—our boy Newton was in exactly the right position. It hit him smack on that part of his bean that retaliated with the theory of gravity."

"You don't give him much credit."

"I give him a lot of credit. I rate him *summa cum laude* in spades."

"But you've just finished saying it was nothing more than luck."

"The luck is maybe thirty per cent. The other seventy is diligence and gumption, adding up to long hours and hard work."

"Or call it willpower."

"Yes, that's probably what it is. It amounts to willpower."

She opened her mouth to say something, then decided to hold it back.

He nodded, as though she'd put it into words. He said, "I'm strictly a bush leaguer when it comes to that."

"I wasn't thinking—"

"You were thinking there isn't a chance in the world that I'll do anything with this theory. I mean this theory of the life span that tells people they can't ever know how much time they've got. And of course you're right. I'll never develop the theory, I'll never put it on paper, as Newton did, I'm too lazy for that. Only thing I might do is use it as a guidepost."

She was leaning forward intently, a look of fervent hopefulness in her eyes.

He went on with it, talking more to himself than to her. "A guidepost that says, You don't know how much time you've got. You only know you're here, and while you're here you might as well make the most of it. Make the best of it. And try to be nice about it. That's the most important thing. Be nice."

"Oh, good," she breathed. "That's awfully good. Keep thinking that way."

"Well, I'll give it a try."

"Will you make it a resolution?"

"I guess it's something along that line."

The waiter arrived with the figs in cream and the silver-covered plates, the swan-necked coffeepot. He put his napkin on his lap, smiling at Cora and seeing something maternal in her expression as she looked at the food set before him. And then their eyes met and without sound he said to her, I'm your boy and you're my girl, and no matter how much hell we create for each other, there are always moments like this when the unity is so real and you're so poignantly precious to me. It's so far away from obligation when it's like this, so softly and tenderly and yet with a kind of revelry we exult in our togetherness. Yes, we're really celebrating and it doesn't need confetti or balloons or the funny little hats. When it's like this it's something too idyllic. Like one time I remember...

He remembered one time when it had been like

this, a time that caressed his memory with such soft, sweet tenderness that it brought a sigh from his lips. It was in the summertime a couple of years ago. It was the beginning of a weekend and New York was stifling and they'd decided to join some friends at a mountain resort in the Adirondacks. But they never got there. The car developed trouble in the fuel pump and there were no mechanics around. He was starting to worry about it and she smiled and told him not to worry. She pointed to a lake nearby and a field of daisies and clover and she said, "It's nice here. It's so nice and quiet, and we can stay at that little motel we saw down the road. It's only a mile back. And while you're checking in I'll be calling the AAA."

So that night and the next night they stayed at the little motel. In the daytime they swam in the lake and walked in the field and picked flowers. Nothing exciting happened, but it was a really wonderful weekend. It was forty-eight hours of floating away from everything and having only each other, feeling so near to each other that they talked mostly with their eyes, saying in unison, You're all there is for me, there's nothing else I really care about, only you.

There were other times like that, but he remembered that time especially as he looked at her now and said to her with his eyes, You're all there is for me.

For then and now and forever, he said to her with his eyes, you're my Grecian goddess who floats me up and away from a world jam-packed with stumbling blocks. Oh, Cora, my adorable, try to see it through with me while I give it another try. I'll try so hard this time to stop the drinking and the rattle-brained thinking and all the carrying-on. I'll really try this time. I'll try.

She was nodding slowly, and smiling. And then, her voice soft, she told him to start eating his breakfast.

It was excellent food and he went at it somewhat greedily. In very little time the plates were empty. Cora poured more coffee for him and for herself. They sat there sipping the coffee and smoking.

She said, "Look out there, through the window. Look at that sunshine."

"It's like summertime," he said.

"It must be freezing in New York."

"That's a comfortable thought."

"But rather selfish," she admitted. "We mustn't wish bad weather on them."

"Let's get some of that sun," he said. "Let's get out and do something today. What should we do?"

"I don't know. What would you like?"

"Well, we haven't seen much of the island."

"Or the city either, for that matter."

"Oh, I've seen the city," he said lightly. "I've seen quite a bit of the city."

"Would you like to go sailing? They have boats leaving from the hotel."

"All right," he said. "Let's go sailing."

She was getting up from the table. "I'll go up to the room and change into slacks. Won't take me a minute."

He sat there watching her as she walked out of the dining room. Now the dining room was getting busy as guests came in for lunch. Some of them smiled and nodded to him and he returned the pleasant greetings, feeling glad that he could do it without forcing it. He told himself he was beginning to feel at home in the Laurel Rock, more of a participant than an observer. It was a soothing thought, and he felt friendly toward everyone at the other tables. And then it occurred to him that there was more to it than that; he was starting to feel sort of friendly toward himself.

I guess that's all it takes, he thought. It's so easy to be accepted if you can accept yourself. Now if you can only keep it going like this, keep it steady on a road aiming up instead of down, there's maybe a chance you'll make the grade. Or at least be able to look in a mirror and see a teammate rather than an opponent. He was dwelling on that idea when a hand fell lightly on his shoulder.

He turned his head and looked up. The man stood there smiling down at him. It was a soft smile. It was very soft, almost gentle. But instantly the meaning of it was clear and hard and terribly cold, like the all too real transparency of a cake of ice.

The man was a Jamaican. His skin was the color of tobacco. He was on the slim side, of medium height, and it was evident that he had some Caucasian blood in him, for his hair was straight and his nose was thin, rather narrow at the base. His lips were very thin and altogether he gave the impression that his diet was mostly green vegetables. Even his eyes were the blunt and dry green of raw spinach.

He was attired inexpensively yet neatly. His cotton shirt was spotless, the gray tie knotted accurately. The suit was a cotton-and-rayon mixture, plain dark gray. It looked as though it had been pressed quite recently, and probably with a flatiron; the sleeves and trousers were creased blade-sharp. In sum, the man's appearance showed he was dressed for what he deemed to be a very special occasion.

He went on giving Bevan the soft smile, saying very softly, "Pardon me, sir. You are Mr.—?"

Bevan didn't say anything.

"My name is Nathan Joyner."

"What is it? What can I do for you?"

The Jamaican circled to the other side of the table. "May I sit down?"

"Sure."

Joyner seated himself. He said, "You remember me?"

"No," Bevan said. "I've never seen you before."

"You saw me last night," Joyner said.

Bevan told himself the only thing to do was keep quiet.

"On Barry Street," the Jamaican said. "At Winnie's Place."

All right, he thought. Make it fast. Get it over with.

"Or perhaps I should put it this way," Joyner said. "You do not remember seeing me. You were somewhat intoxicated."

The man's accent was British, and Bevan said to himself, This one's a businessman. Maybe he took a business course at Cambridge or some good school in London. Whatever school he went to, he must have majored in merchandising.

He heard himself saying, "I'm not intoxicated now. I'm thinking quite clearly now."

"Splendid," Joyner said. "This matter calls for a maximum of clear thinking." He leaned forward slightly. "You're probably aware of my reason for coming here?"

Bevan shrugged. "It isn't too difficult to guess."

"There's no need to guess," Joyner said. "You know I wouldn't be here if I hadn't seen what happened in the alley."

It was quiet for some moments.

And then Joyner said, "I saw it from the doorway."

"What were you doing in the doorway?"

"Just standing there watching."

"You knew he was trying to rob me?"

Joyner nodded.

"Why didn't you try to stop it?" Bevan asked.

"It was none of my affair," Joyner said. "I make it a practice not to interfere in these things."

"You do? How come you're interfering now?"

"This isn't interference. This is merely a discussion of the issue."

"All right, I'm willing to discuss it. No reason why I shouldn't discuss it. You want some coffee?"

"No, thank you," Joyner said. He noticed Cora's empty cup on the table. He gave Bevan an inquiring look.

"My wife," Bevan said. "She went up to our room to change her clothes. She's getting into slacks. We're going sailing."

"It's a fine day for sailing."

"It certainly is," Bevan said. "It's a perfect day for sailing. By the way, my name is Bevan—James Bevan."

"I'm pleased to know you, Mr. Bevan."

They were smiling pleasantly at each other. Then Bevan widened his smile just a little and said, "How'd you know where to find me?"

"I assumed you'd be here at the Laurel Rock. Most tourists are registered at the Laurel Rock."

Bevan glanced around at the other tables. Now all the tables were taken and the waiters were very busy. He said, "They're having a big season."

"Yes, the rooms are always filled this time of the year," Joyner said. "It's the climate, I guess. You like the climate here, Mr. Bevan?"

"Very much. It's really a wonderful climate."

"How long are you staying?"

"A few weeks."

"I hope you have a pleasant stay."

"Thank you, Mr. Joyner."

Again, they were smiling at each other. Joyner said, "I'm sure you'll have a pleasant stay. It's so easy to enjoy yourself in Jamaica. That is, when you're staying at a fine hotel like the Laurel Rock."

Bevan didn't say anything.

And Joyner went on, "It's really an excellent hotel. Of course, it's only for those who can afford it."

Here we go, Bevan thought. Now we get some Dun and Bradstreet. Or maybe he's trying to get me upset, get me immobilized so that when he throws it at me, it'll knock me flat. Well, whatever it is, I wish he'd quit fooling around and come out with it. This waiting on edge is like watching the dentist preparing to drill. Let's see if we can pull him in a little.

He went on smiling at the Jamaican. He said, "It's all a matter of luck, I guess. Some have it and some don't."

"You have it," Joyner said.

He shrugged. "To some extent."

"Can you be more specific?"

"You mean you want a financial statement?"

"It would help," Joyner said. And then his smile became thinner. "How much can you afford to pay?"

"For what? What are you selling?"

"A lapse of memory," Joyner said. "I'm willing to forget what I saw last night."

Bevan laughed lightly, soundlessly. "All right, Nathan. You want to play checkers, we'll play checkers." He placed his hands flat on the table and leaned forward and said, "Can you prove you saw anything?"

Joyner nodded. Now his face was expressionless. He said, "I'm in possession of a broken bottle. There's blood on it. And of course it will show your fingerprints."

"Very good, Nathan. You have something there. Only thing is, it adds up to nothing. If you open your mouth and they pick me up, I'll just tell them the truth. I'll claim the man was trying to rob me."

"You think they'll accept that?"

"Of course they'll accept it. Why shouldn't they?"

"Several reasons," Joyner said. And then he smiled again. His spinach-green eyes were narrowing very slowly, as though wanting to put it all in shadow, his eyelids coming down like a curtain on the living object he was looking at.

Bevan could feel it coming down on him. It was really like a curtain coming down and all at once it had nothing to do with Nathan Joyner; it was caused by something inside him. There were words printed on the curtain, the same words he'd seen on the billboards displayed against the blackness of fitful slumber. Again he read the announcement: "This man destroyed a human being and it wasn't an accident, and don't believe him when he claims self-defense...."

He heard Joyner saying, "If this ever gets to a court-room, you won't have a chance. They'll send you to the gallows."

Chapter Six

Bevan was leaning back in his chair. He had his head turned sideways and he was gazing vacantly at nothing in particular.

The quiet went on for some moments and then Joyner said, "What it amounts to, I'm giving you a chance to remain alive."

Bevan grinned.

"Did I say something funny?" Joyner murmured.

"Hilarious," Bevan said. He put the grin on the Jamaican. Without sound he said, Yes, it's really hilarious, Nathan. A couple of nights ago I was playing with the idea of doing away with myself. Now you come along and maybe you'll save me the trouble.

Joyner bit very lightly at the side of his mouth. He said, "Perhaps you don't understand. Or maybe you don't care."

"I guess that's it," Bevan said aloud to himself. "I just don't care."

The Jamaican frowned. It was a clinical frown. He said, "I must admit, Mr. Bevan, you confuse me."

"Don't knock yourself out."

Joyner studied him. The clinical frown deepened in Joyner's brow. For the better part of a minute there was no sound at the table. Then footsteps moved in and they both looked up and saw Cora standing there. She sent an inquiring smile to the Jamaican and back to Bevan. The Jamaican had risen from his chair and was nodding politely, waiting to be introduced. Bevan said, "Cora, this is Mr. Joyner. Mrs. Bevan."

They murmured salutations and sat down. Bevan said, "Mr. Joyner is a friend of mine. He's a very dear friend of mine. He's trying awfully hard to help me."

Cora didn't say anything. She only winced slightly.

Bevan said, "Go on and tell her, Mr. Joyner. Tell her all about it."

"It's rather difficult—"

"Oh, go ahead," Bevan said. "She can take it."

"Yes, I can take it," Cora said.

Joyner gave a little sigh. He looked at Cora and said, "Has your husband told you what happened while he was out last night?"

She nodded.

"I told her it was self-defense," Bevan said. And then, smiling at Cora, "Our friend Mr. Joyner has doubts about that."

"No, that wasn't what I said," the Jamaican murmured. "I said that all the doubt would come from the authorities. I told you there's very little chance they'd accept your explanation."

Bevan was grinning again. "You see the way it is? He has it figured. He has it all figured out very nicely."

Cora sat there stiffly. "Who is this man? What does he want?"

"He's a businessman," Bevan said. "He wants money."

She looked at the Jamaican. "All right," she said. "I'm listening."

Joyner leaned his elbows on the table, his hands

clasped together under his chin. His eyes were focused on Bevan's necktie. But he spoke as though Bevan weren't there. He said, "If they get him, they'll hang him, I've already told him that, but it didn't seem to make an impression. Perhaps it impresses you, Mrs. Bevan. You appear to be a sensible woman."

"You bet she is," Bevan said. "She's very sensible. I ought to know, I—"

"Be quiet, James. Please be quiet."

"O.K. But where's the waiter? I want a drink."

"Not now."

"Just one. Tell you what, we'll all have one. Come on, let's all have a drink."

"Please," she said. "Oh, James. Please."

"Then later." He shrugged. "I'll have one later."

She turned to the Jamaican. "You were saying?"

"I was anticipating the reaction of the authorities," Joyner said. "That is, if your husband is apprehended. Of course, I'm hoping he won't be apprehended. They'd have such a strong case against him."

"They'd have no case at all," Cora said. "He was only trying to protect himself."

Joyner shook his head. "It doesn't jell, Mrs. Bevan. For one thing he failed to report the matter. He actually fled from the scene."

"Who wouldn't? It was a dreadful ordeal. It threw him into a state of shock."

"Granted." Joyner nodded slowly. "But the fact remains, he can't prove self-defense. The other man didn't have a weapon."

"The hell he didn't," Bevan mumbled.

Cora looked at him. Her eyes urged him to go on with it, to lift himself up from nothingness and come back to solid ground.

"He had a blackjack," Bevan said.

"The authorities don't know that." And then a slow thin smile drifted across Joyner's mouth.

"He had a blackjack and they'll find it," Cora said.

"They'll never find it," Joyner murmured.

Her eyes began to widen.

"You get the picture?" Bevan said to her. "You see what's happening here?"

She was staring at the Jamaican, seeing the spinach-green eyes smiling back at her.

Then Bevan was saying, "Our friend here is a real engineer, all right. He's certainly a cute one." He grinned at the Jamaican. "Oh, you cute bastard, you."

Joyner looked at Cora. "What's the matter with your husband? Is he sick?"

"Sure I'm sick." Bevan widened the grin and it became a grimace. "I'm sick and it feels great."

"You're not sick." Cora told him. She spoke slowly and precisely. "I won't have you saying you're sick."

"All right, then, it's the world that's sick. The whole world is sick and I'm in fine shape. How's that?"

And again Joyner was frowning clinically, saying to Cora, "He seems to be out of contact."

"Out of contact, my foot." Bevan grinned at him. "I'm skipping along right beside you, Nathan. I have all your moves down pat. Number one, you have the broken bottle to prove I did it. And two, you picked up the blackjack so I'd have no evidence to show he was armed. From there on in it's a breeze for you. There are witnesses who'll testify they saw me in that house, saw me drinking rum and getting a load on. And then of course there's your testimony. It'll probably be something freakish—I invited the man to come out with me and he came out but then he changed his mind about it and I became irritated and grabbed the first thing I could put my hands on."

Joyner was nodding very slowly. "That's it."

"But it's a lie." Cora was breathing hard. "It's such a filthy lie."

"What does he care?" Bevan gave a little laugh. "Look at him."

She looked at the face of the Jamaican. The green eyes flickered and it was a mixture of ice and flame. Then it was all ice.

And Joyner said, "We can settle this matter for five thousand dollars."

Cora took a very deep breath and held it.

Bevan said, "Make it five cents and I'll talk business."

Then it was quiet. Joyner was sitting relaxed, his arms loose at his sides. Bevan leaned very low over the table, aiming a vacant and somewhat idiotic grin at the silver coffeepot. Cora had her head lowered, her face cupped in her hands.

Finally Joyner said, "I'm waiting. I think you ought to make up your mind here and now. You won't have another chance."

"You're terrific," Bevan said, still grinning at the coffeepot. "You ought to be selling insurance."

"This is insurance." Joyner smiled at him. "This is the finest insurance you'll ever buy."

"Who says I'm buying it?"

"Oh, you'll buy it, all right. I'm quite sure you'll buy it."

Cora took her hands from her face. Her eyes were shut tightly and then she opened them and said, "We can't afford five thousand dollars. We can't come anywhere near that."

Joyner smiled pleasantly. "What's the best you can do?"

She looked at Bevan. She waited for him to say something. But it wasn't any use. He was concentrating on the coffeepot, its silver roundness giving him a distorted reflection of his grinning face. Then he changed it to a sullen frown, and then back to a grin. He was making faces at himself in the spherical shiny silver of the coffeepot.

Joyner said, "It's up to you, Mrs. Bevan. I can't do anything with him."

"Neither can I," she said before she could hold it back. She pressed her fingers hard against her forehead. She said, "We'll give you a thousand dollars."

Joyner shook his head.

"We can't give you more than a thousand," she said. "You must understand, we're not very wealthy people."

"Make it two thousand," Joyner said.

"We can't." Her voice strained with pleading. "We really can't."

"Let's investigate that," the Jamaican murmured. "What kind of work does your husband do?"

"I'm an exterminator," Bevan said. "I go around exterminating. It's a lot of fun."

"He sells investment securities," Cora said.

"That's only a part-time job," Bevan mumbled, still gazing at his reflection in the coffeepot. "Actually, I'm a circus performer. On the tightrope. It's a special kind of tightrope. It goes around in circles."

"Does he always talk like that?" Joyner asked.

"Only on off days," Bevan whispered confidentially, cupping his hand at the side of his mouth. "I have these off days seven days a week."

Joyner sighed. He glanced pityingly at Cora. It was genuine pity. He said to her, "It's too bad. I know you don't have an easy life."

"Oh, dry up," Bevan told him. "Go take a walk somewhere and dry up."

"I can see what a problem you have," Joyner said to Cora. "Can't you do something for him?"

Bevan let out a hooting laugh. It was very loud. People at other tables turned their heads and looked. Then they saw who it was and they shrugged. Someone said, "He's at it again."

Cora had her head lowered. Her eyes were shut tightly.

Joyner was saying, "You carry a heavy burden, Mrs. Bevan. I don't want to make it more difficult for you. But there's nothing else I can do. It's a matter of drastic necessity. I'm a poor man. I'm really very poor."

She looked at him. "Are you trying to justify your position?"

"In a way." The Jamaican returned her level gaze. "It's a matter of economics. It's the old law of supply and demand. You want your husband to stay alive and I'm supplying the guarantee. You can't buy it from anyone else."

"That simplifies the issue," Bevan remarked to no one in particular. "That simplifies it very nicely."

Joyner went on looking at Cora. He said, "Can you make it fifteen hundred?"

"All right," she said.

"I want it in pound notes."

"All right." She sounded very tired.

"Can you handle it now?"

"I imagine so," she said. "My husband and I have a joint bank account. I'll go to the desk and make out a check. It'll take a little time while they clear it with New York."

"I'll wait," Joyner said.

Cora got up from the table. She was trying to keep her shoulders straight as she walked across the dining room toward the lobby. Bevan had his head raised and he was watching her and thinking, Now there's a pretty number. She looks so dainty and delicate in slacks. Really charming in a quietly elegant sort of way. Not many of them can wear slacks like that. She wears them so gracefully. And look at her pale-gold hair. Yes, that's quite a number and I wouldn't mind having a date with that. Maybe I can make a date with her to go sailing. It's such a nice day for sailing.

Chapter Seven

Then later she came back to the table where Joyner was smoking a cigarette and Bevan was drinking a gin-and-tonic. She handed Joyner a thick envelope. She murmured, "Please don't count it here," and he smiled and said, "Of course not." Then he got up and walked out of the dining room. In a few minutes he came back and said to her, "It's all there." He saw the way she was looking at him and he said, "You needn't worry, Mrs. Bevan. I won't be coming here again." She didn't say anything. Joyner said, "Goodbye, Mrs. Bevan." She was watching Bevan as he worked on the gin-and-tonic and she had her hand pressed to her mouth. Bevan looked up and grinned at her, then grinned at Joyner, and then he went back to the gin-and-tonic. Joyner shook his head slowly and walked away.

Some moments passed and then Cora said, "I don't feel well. I'm going up to the room."

"Oh, you feel all right," Bevan said. "Stay here."

"I have a headache. And I'm tired. I'm terribly tired and I want to go up to the room."

"You don't want to go sailing?"

"No, I don't want to go sailing," she said. She watched him while he sipped from the glass. "You know what I really want to do?" She spoke very quietly. "I want to throw up."

"Oh, don't say that. It isn't that bad."

"Isn't it?"

He didn't reply. He took a long gulp from the glass. It was a very tall glass and now he had it almost empty.

She said, "You realize how much we gave him? We gave him fifteen hundred dollars."

He shrugged. He wasn't looking at her. His eyes were focused on the glass, measuring the amount of liquor that remained.

"Fifteen hundred dollars," she said. "And you don't care. You're not the least bit bothered. If we gave him every cent we had it still wouldn't bother you."

Bevan shrugged again.

And she said, "I'm wondering if you've reached the point where nothing can bother you."

Then he looked at her.

She was breathing in hard through her teeth. It made a slight whistling noise. She said, "We couldn't afford that fifteen hundred dollars. You know that, don't you?"

"Oh, let's forget it."

"No." She shook her head emphatically. "Not this time."

"You said you were going up to the room. Why don't you go?"

"First I'll say what's on my mind. Unless you prefer that I hold it back. The way I'm always holding it back. Biting on it. Choking on it."

"Then let it out, for Christ's sake. What is it?"

"I want you to do something. You're falling apart and you'll just have to do something."

"Like what? Take pills? Shots in the arm?"

"Just get a grip on yourself, that's all."

"That's all," he echoed, mimicking her. "As if it's a routine matter. On the order of getting a haircut."

"You can do it."

"Oh, sure, I can do anything. I can outdance Gene Kelly and outbox Gavilan and outgolf Ben Hogan. Just give me time to prove it. Give me a little time."

"To do what? To ruin yourself completely? To ruin me?"

He looked at the glass of gin-and-tonic. He said to the glass, "You hear that? You hear what the lady says?"

"Look at me." She was talking through her teeth, straining to keep her voice low. "I'm talking to you. Can't you give me a sensible answer?"

"Frankly, no." He lifted the glass and held it to his mouth until it was empty. He set it down very carefully and studied it for a long moment, then said, "It needs refilling, that's what it needs."

Cora stood up. She started to say something and couldn't get it out. She turned away from the table and hurried out of the dining room. There was something frenzied in the way she hurried, and he got up and started to follow her. Then he changed his mind about that and went back to the table. He beckoned to a passing waiter and ordered a refill on the gin-and-tonic.

An hour later he was still sitting there, drinking slowly and methodically and not thinking about anything in particular. The tables were empty now. The waiters had cleared off all the dishes and were busy wiping the bread crumbs off the chairs and sweeping the floor. Several times they bypassed Bevan's table, their eyes giving him a polite hint that he was in their way and he ought to do his drinking in the bar. Finally the headwaiter came over and made it a courteous request. Bevan lifted himself from the chair and went out of the dining room. He crossed the lobby and entered the bar. All the stools were occupied, and he looked around for a table. There were several empty tables, and he was moving toward the nearest one when he saw them at a small table for two near the far wall.

They didn't see him. They faced each other across tall frosted glasses of something green-orange, something that looked like a fruit drink. They hadn't touched the drinks and they were concentrating on each other. Cora was saying something and the man was nodding seriously. Then the man said something and Cora nodded. Then they both smiled.

Bevan smiled also. Episode Two, he said without sound. Continued from yesterday. He aimed the smile at the man's slightly flattened nose and carrot-colored hair. At a nearby table some people were getting up and he edged his way in. He sat down and quickly picked up the large drink menu, keeping it in front of his face. He heard Cora saying, "—that's very kind of you, Mr. Atkinson."

"It wasn't a compliment," the man said. "It was a statement of fact. You're an exceptionally pretty girl."

"Girl? That was a long time ago. I've been married nine years."

"Really? It doesn't show. Or maybe—"

"Maybe what?"

"Your eyes. It shows in your eyes."

"Even when I'm smiling?"

"Yes," the man said. "Even when you're smiling. It's such a weary smile, it tells me so much about you."

"You do this often, Mr. Atkinson?"

"Do what?"

"Read stories in people's eyes."

"No," the man said. "I've never done it before. I've never been sufficiently interested. That is, until now."

"But the point is, I'm married."

"That isn't the point at all. There's only one issue involved here, and I'm quite sure you know what it is."

"I wish you hadn't said that."

"It needed saying. There are many things that need saying."

Then it was quiet at the table for two. Bevan kept the drink menu in front of his face. He was thinking, She's really attracted to him. Or maybe it's just that she needs something to lean on and he happens to be around. You prefer to believe that? I think you better keep tuned to this program. It'll let you know the score one way or another. I wish I could see her face right now. She's sitting there so quietly; I don't like that quiet.

The man was saying, "You can't deny it, Cora."

"It's Mrs. Bevan."

"No, it's Cora. I insist it's Cora."

"That isn't quite proper."

"I knew you'd say that. You make a big thing of proper behavior, don't you?"

"Yes, I do. I think restraint is rather important."

"In its place," the man said. "But this isn't the place. This isn't the time."

"I'd better go."

"You know you won't go," the man said. "You know you want to sit here and talk to me."

"Not about that."

"We've got to talk about that," the man said. "There's really nothing else for us to talk about."

Again it was quiet. And then Bevan heard her saying, "You're really serious about this."

"It's more than that. I'm determined."

"That sounds almost aggressive."

"I don't care how it sounds. If I thought there were nothing happening here, I wouldn't attempt to carry it further. And certainly I wouldn't be expressing my feelings. But there's something happening and you know it, we both know it."

"Mr. Atkinson—"

"We knew it yesterday, at the swimming pool, when we talked about this and that, just making conversation. It was books and the theatre and travel and so forth. All very quiet and calm on the surface. But the undercurrent—"

"I wish you wouldn't."

"Why not? Are you afraid to hear it?"

She didn't reply.

The man said, "At one time I served in the Navy. I was an officer in command of a patrol boat. For three years it carried me through various campaigns in the Pacific. It was a fine boat and it taught me quite a few lessons. There's one in particular I've never forgotten. It goes something like this: When you know precisely what you want to do, go ahead and do it."

"That's a bold philosophy, Mr. Atkinson."

"It's bold because it's based on truth," the man said. Then his voice was a lunge of sound: "I want to take you away from him."

He means it, Bevan thought. He isn't playing around, he really means it.

Cora was saying, "I don't know what to tell you. It's all happening so quickly. There's been no indication—"

"It was indicated quite clearly when we first met. I saw you and you saw me and that was it."

"Aren't you taking a lot for granted?"

"Not at all. It happens to be a fact. An irrevocable fact."

"Please," she said. "Please don't look at me like that."

"There's no other way I can look at you."

"No...." Her voice faltered and fell away. "We mustn't. Oh, I can't manage this." She sounded as though she were talking aloud to herself. "It's too much for me. At any other time I'd know what to think, what to say. But not now."

"Would you mind straightening me out on that?"

"Don't ask me to explain it."

They were quiet for some moments, and then the man said, "Maybe it doesn't need explaining. Maybe I know."

Sure he knows, Bevan thought. Anyone would know. Anyone with eyes. They take one look at Mr. and Mrs.

Bevan and they know what kind of marriage it is. Or at least they see part of the story. Now he's seeing her face and getting the rest of the story. Or no, not entirely. Just her side of it. So what are you supposed to do? Jump up on a platform and state your side of it? They'd roll in the aisles, brother. They'd sign you up for the Colgate Comedy Hour.

He heard the man saying, "I saw you when you came walking out of the dining room. You left him there sitting at the table. There was a greenish look on your face when you stepped into the elevator. I think I know why you went up to your room. You were sick to your stomach, weren't you?"

She didn't answer.

The man said, "Why does he drink so much?"

"He can't help it."

"You mean he won't make the effort. Isn't that what you mean?"

"I'm not sure. I don't know what's the matter with him."

"I do," the man said.

"Oh, please," she said. "You've met him only once. You're scarcely acquainted with him."

"That makes me all the more perceptive." The man paused to let it hang there for a moment. And then, "He's suffering from a condition known as lack of backbone."

Bevan winced slightly. He didn't realize he'd winced.

"It's a pity," the man said. "Not for him. For you."

"There's nothing I can do about it."

"Yes, there is," the man said. "Most certainly there's something you can do about it."

She was quiet. And Bevan thought, He's getting it across to her, he's really selling it to her. Well, he caught her at the right time.

He heard the man saying, "I think at this point I'd better give you some statistics. I'm thirty-nine years old. I've been divorced for three years. She gets four hundred dollars a month alimony. Or rather, charity. The court didn't order it. I give her the money because I feel sorry for her. She's really in a bad way. She's pathologically incapable of remaining faithful to any one man. When I caught her, I broke her jaw. I've always felt bad about that."

There was a pause. And then she said, "You have children?"

"Three boys. Ages eight and nine and twelve. They're in military school. Of course they're in my custody. I make a point of seeing them at least once a month. They're fine boys, and they make excellent grades in school. I wish I could see them more often, but my work requires a lot of traveling."

"What do you do?"

"I'm a mining engineer. Mostly copper. There's a big demand for copper and they pay me rather nicely."

"I'm not interested in your income, Mr. Atkinson."

"I know you're not. If I thought you were, I wouldn't be telling you. It amounts to around forty thousand a year."

Very nice, Bevan thought. That's a fair working wage. And it's a cinch he doesn't throw it away. The tone of his voice tells me that. The tone of his voice tells me many things. It's a deep thick baritone and it goes along with that slightly flattened nose. So instead of night clubs it's early to bed and instead of the race track it's fishing and hunting. And books, too. Probably Steinbeck and Melville, maybe some of Walter Scott, although I'd say he's a little too sophisticated for Scott. But not pseudo-sophisticated. Not with the embroidery that always lets you know there's nothing underneath. This one has plenty underneath.

Hey, what are you doing? You rooting for him? No, I think what it adds up to, you're rooting for her. That's why you're sizing him up. You want to be sure she'll have something worthwhile. So I hope you fill the bill, Mr. Atkinson. I hope you'll be nice to her and make her happy. She's a good girl and she merits some happiness, considering the fact she's had so little of it.

What I think this calls for is another gin-and-tonic. Or it might be a good idea to fill the swimming pool with gin and dive in. But gin doesn't quite fit this mood. What would you say would fit this mood? The diving part of it is fine. Let's make it a high dive, say a few hundred feet up with rocks at the bottom, a collection of nice sharp rocks. Only thing is, that kind of stunt takes nerve. And as the man says, you haven't got it, brother. As he says, the condition is known as a lack of backbone. Let's call for a show of hands on that one. The ayes have it.

He heard a scraping of chairs at the table for two. Then he heard the footsteps going away from the table. He lowered the drink menu and saw them walking out together. As they moved through the doorway leading from the bar to the lobby, Cora's face was in profile. The man was talking to her and she was deeply engrossed in what he was saying. Her lips were slightly parted and her expression was passive and somewhat dreamy, almost childlike. Then her shoulders drooped just a little, very little, and yet it seemed more emphatic than that. It was like a gesture of surrender.

Am I giving in? she asked herself. Am I really giving in and saying yes to this man? I don't know. I'm not sure of anything right now. I'm not even sure of where we are, or where he's taking me. Where is he taking me?

They were walking, across the lobby. He guided her to the side door leading out toward the swimming pool area. Then they were out there and she blinked tightly in the hot yellow flashing of the Caribbean sunlight. The swimming pool area was crowded and she heard him saying, "Let's get away from this mob. Let's walk in the garden." Without sound she said, Garden? What garden? And he said, "They have a wonderful garden here. The flowers are really something to see."

But I don't want to see, she thought. I don't want the garden. I want to stay away from the garden. She tried to say it aloud but it was as though she had no voice. All she could do was walk along at his side, moving toward a velvety lawn and then across the lawn and onto a pebbly path that rimmed the circular arrangement of shrubs and flowers. It was a large garden and a section of it was sunken, a flight of stone steps going down through the middle of a varicolored slope that glittered like a collection of precious gems. This section was the rock garden. The rocks were silver-green and silver-pink and amber-yellow, and the flowers were purple and dark blue and very bright blue and bright orange. Some of the larger rocks were sprigged with laurel.

"—gives this place its name," he was saying. "You see there? The laurel on the rocks?" For a moment he stepped away from her to have a closer look. He said, "It's bay laurel. Comes from southern Europe."

But she didn't hear. At that instant she'd lost her balance on the steps, and as she started to fall he pivoted quickly and grabbed her. His thick fingers encircled her arms, and as he pulled her upright she sagged against him. Then she straightened and he released her and they looked at each other. She felt the pressure of his eyes burning into her face. It was like liquid fire going into her. It boiled in her brain and in her blood and she thought, I'm getting dizzy, I'm getting so dizzy....

But it can't be that, she said to herself. It's the sun, it's such a terribly hot sun. I ought to have a parasol. Yes, it would be all right if I had a parasol, because it's only the sun. But stop it, please. Stop looking at me like that.

Then they were walking together down the stone

steps and there was space between them but it was
as though he were touching her. It was actually as
though he were holding her, gripping her, hugging her,
his thick fingers squeezing her, kneading her flesh,
melting her. She heard a voice that could have been
his voice but she knew it wasn't his voice; it was
coming from far away and it was saying, "Don't get
yourself dirty." She spoke back to the voice, her nerves
taut and straining with all the defiance she could
summon, saying, Leave me alone, leave me alone.
Can't you leave me alone? Can't you understand? I
want this. I need it. I know how much I need it and
I've got to have it. But of course you can't have it,
you're afraid of it. But why? Why are you so afraid?
Well, it's filthy, it's shameful and dreadful. It's contam-
inating, that's what it is. You can't even do it with the
man whose ring you wear. For some reason...

For some unearthly, ghastly reason...

She shivered. And then for a moment her mind was
a lens focused on time and she was seeing through a
very long tunnel filled with the darkness of years and
years and more years. It's back there, she thought.
Something happened back there. It took hold of me
and never let go. It's like clawing fingers in my brain,
the fingers gripping the thoughts and twisting the
thoughts to choke off all growth. Yes, that's what
it's done to you. It's kept you from growing. But what
does that mean? You know what it means. It means
you're not a woman, not really. You're just a frightened
little girl.

I won't be frightened, she said to herself. I'm

twenty-nine years old and I'm reasonably intelligent, at least sufficiently intelligent to see it for what it is. Well then, what is it?

Well, whatever it is, it's nothing to cause fright. Certainly there's no reason to be frightened of this man Atkinson. Sure, he's on the rugged side, and I think underneath that healthy wholesome Boy Scout manner he's got some nasty bully in him. For instance, that business about punching his wife in the face and breaking her jaw. He didn't need to mention that, but he seemed to enjoy mentioning it. But all the same, I'm sure he's more gentleman than otherwise and there won't be any trouble. Let's start from that premise, shall we?

But I want it, she said to herself.

No, you don't mean that.

But yes, I do. I want him to—

Now stop that, she told herself. Stop that once and for all.

All right, I'll stop it. I'll try to stop it.

She said aloud, "I wish I had a parasol."

"Yes," he said. "It's really blazing out here."

"It's a scorcher," she said. And then, her voice somewhat unsteady, "Let's— I mean, let's go back."

"There's some shade over there." He was pointing toward a collection of shrubs and trees. "Maybe there's a bench and you can rest for a while. At any rate, you can cool off."

They'd arrived at the base of the stone steps and now they were moving toward the shrubs and trees. There was a narrow path slicing through thick foliage going toward the trees and she was walking in front of him and feeling his presence very close behind her. She was telling herself he was too close, then telling herself the path was too narrow, the foliage was too thick. She shivered again. She told herself to stop shivering and keep walking and she walked slowly and steadily along the path, which made a turn and turned again and went between the trees to show her the small pond. It was a very small pond placed in there among the bushes. It was a goldfish pond.

She let out a racking cry and started to run. Then she collapsed. As he lifted her from the ground she was gasping and saying, "Take me away—take me away from here."

A waiter came to the table and said to Bevan, "What will it be, sir?"

"Anything. You name it."

"Something with rum?"

"Rum," he murmured musingly. He looked at the dark face of the waiter. "What kind of rum?"

"The best, sir. We serve only the best."

"I don't want the best. I want the worst."

The waiter smiled patiently.

"The worst," Bevan said. "The brand that's labeled 'For Hopeless Wrecks Only.' "

"I'm afraid we don't serve that here, sir."

"You're damn right you don't serve it here. Your customers here are decent, wholesome, respectable people. Correct?"

"Correct, sir."

"So there you have it," Bevan said. "That lets me out."

He stood up, smiling pleasantly at the waiter. He took out his wallet and handed the waiter a dollar bill.

"But really, sir—"

"Hold onto it," he said. "Keep it for a souvenir. A going-away present."

"You mean you're checking out, sir?"

"With bells on." He gave the waiter an amiable pat on the shoulder and walked out of the bar and through the lobby to the main exit, facing Harbour Street. At the outer gate some taxi drivers were clustered, and as he approached they flocked around him, all of them talking fast and each pointing to his taxi as though it had more to offer than the others. He climbed into the nearest taxi, and as the driver moved in behind the wheel, he said, "Winnie's Place."

The driver turned and gaped at him.

"You heard me," he told the driver. "I said Winnie's Place."

"Excuse me, Mr. Captain. But are you quite certain—"

"Yes, I'm quite certain."

"But Mr. Captain—"

"Say look, you want this fare or don't you?"

The driver faced the windshield and started the engine.

Chapter Eight

There was considerable traffic and the taxi moved slowly, its engine stalling every now and then as it came to jolting stops at blocked intersections.

This taxi driver wore an old felt hat, his grimy shirt was buttoned at the collar, and his ragged suit was thick cheviot. The temperature was well over a hundred, but it didn't bother him at all. The only visible sign of discomfort was the way he turned his head every now and then to look at Bevan, in the back seat. Bevan was slumped with his head far back, his half-closed eyes gazing up at the roof of the car, his mouth shaping a dim smile. He had a lighted cigarette between his fingers, but he wasn't smoking it. He held it in front of his face and the smoke curled up past his Buddha-like smile. It added up to the appearance of a living incense burner.

The taxi driver was taking another look at him and saying, "You feel all right, Mr. Captain?"

"Wonderful," he murmured. "Just wonderful."

"You sure? You look—"

"Don't tell me how I look. I know how I look."

"If dere is anything I can do—"

"Just take me to Winnie's Place."

The taxi driver shrugged and returned his attention to the wheel. But he was frowning puzzledly, and after some moments he said, "You have some business there?"

"Business?" He let the smile fade away. "Yes, I guess you could call it business."

"In dat house?" The taxi driver was loudly incredulous. "On Barry Street? I must admit, Mr. Captain, you make me very curious."

"That's a trait I have," Bevan murmured. "I go around making people curious."

The taxi driver took another look at him. "You better watch where you're driving," Bevan said mildly. "You're liable to put us through a plate-glass window."

They were stopped at an intersection. There was a long line of cars ahead of them. The taxi driver turned in his seat, facing Bevan and saying, "Do you mind if I make de question?"

"Not at all." Bevan's smile was polite and friendly. "What would you like to know?"

"Why you go to Winnie's Place?"

"That's an easy one," Bevan said. "I'm going there to drink rum."

"But why dere?"

"I like it there."

"You mean de rum? It is all de same rum, Mr. Captain. You can obtain de rum anyplace. Me interested to know why you prefer Winnie's house."

Bevan shrugged. "Maybe it's the decor."

"De what?"

"Nothing," Bevan said. "Let's skip that."

"Barry Street is bad area," the taxi driver said. "It

very bad, Mr. Captain. It street of much notoriety and scandal. Me not recommend it for tourist."

"I'm not a tourist. Not really."

"Den what are you?"

"I'm Mr. Captain," he said. "Captain of a ship that wanders around. Just wanders around, getting lost."

"Me fail to understand."

"Me too." He grinned at the taxi driver.

The Jamaican frowned back at him and said, "It not fair to make de joke wid me."

"It's no joke," he said. "And you can bet your sweet life on that."

The taxi driver was somewhat appeased. "You see, Mr. Captain, me announce dese tings for you own good welfare. Me live in dis city all my life and me know what happens here. Me say to you wid de most of seriousness, you put risk on your shoulders when you go to Barry Street. If me can persuade you—"

"I don't think you can," Bevan said softly.

"But listen, Mr. Captain. Please listen to me—"

"You trying to sell me a longer ride?"

"Believe me, Mr. Captain, it is not dat. Me only attempting to warn you. When you enter Barry Street, you invite all varieties of trouble. Winnie's Place is decidedly a location of much danger. Now me give you de fact to support de statement. Last night at dat house a gentlemon was murdered."

"Really?"

"Yes, and a ghastly thing it was. Dey find he in de alley outside de house. He throat is cut."

"Too bad," Bevan murmured. He pointed toward

the windshield that showed the traffic moving. "We can go now."

The driver turned and faced the wheel. The taxi gave a jolt as he let the clutch out too fast. It jolted again in second gear, but after that he had it going smoothly and for some moments he concentrated on his driving. Then again he turned his head and said, "Stone cold dead wid he throat all cut. A dreadful way for gentlemon to die, don't you tink?"

"Yes," Bevan said. "Whoever did it ought to be—"

"Dey got he," the driver said.

Bevan stiffened slightly. "Got who?"

"De gentlemon who do it," the driver said.

The taxi turned off Harbour onto Duke Street, going north toward Barry.

Bevan threw the half-burned cigarette out the window. Now he was sitting very stiffly on the edge of the seat. He wasn't saying anything.

The driver said, "Dey capture he dis morning, Mr. Captain. Dey go to he house and he in de bed sleeping. It causes me to wonder. Me cannot understand how a gentlemon can sleep after doing a ting like dat."

Bevan's hands were folded tightly in his lap. He was looking down at his crossed thumbs.

"Of course, he make de protest, he say he innocent. But innocent is not de word for dat gentlemon. Dat is bad one, very bad from long time back. A maker of trouble ever since he a child. Dey sent him to de correction school, but he refuse to be corrected, he come out badder than ever, so later dey put he in prison, and again it is waste of de taxpayers' funds. Many times dis gentlemon go to prison, and on each occasion when he come out he meaner and more vicious dan before. But dis time he take it too far. Dey will put de rope around he neck and dat will be de end of he."

Bevan's voice was a low murmur, scarcely audible. "Are they sure they've got the right man?"

"Not de slightest doubt," the taxi driver said. "De case against dis gentlemon is fully established. De victim his hated enemy. It a matter of gambling debts dat de victim could not pay."

"How much was it?"

"Dey say one pound, two shillings."

"That comes to around three dollars."

"Three dollars and eight cents," the taxi driver said.

"That isn't very much."

"You tink not?"

"It's hardly a motive for cutting a man's throat."

The taxi driver gave a dry laugh.

"Did I say something funny?"

"Extremely funny," the taxi driver said. "Captain, you do not understand de economics of dis island."

"Don't give me economics. Give me more on the man they arrested."

"Why you want to know?" The driver threw a glance over his shoulder. "What make you so interested?"

Bevan didn't reply. He spoke aloud to himself. "The motive isn't enough. They need evidence."

"Dey have it."

"How do you know?" Bevan spoke a trifle more loudly. "How do you know so much about it?"

"Me dere when dey bring de gentlemon in. Me driving de taxi past police headquarters, on Queen Street, and me see all de people gathered. It considerable assemblage and much noise and excitement. It very exciting when he make de frantic attempt."

"What attempt?"

"De gentlemon attempt to get away."

"But why?" Again Bevan was talking aloud to himself. "Why would he want to do that?"

The driver shrugged. "It his only chance. He aware he have no chance in de courtroom."

"But if he can prove—" And then of course there was no way to go on with it.

"He can prove nothing," the driver said. "De court do all de proving. First ting dey do, dey tell de jury what a bad character dis gentlemon is. Dey state he long list of crimes, he prison record. Dey bring witnesses to describe de many times he threatened de victim, and if they call me, me will tell dem of occasion when me hear dem quarreling and dis gentlemon he say, 'You pay me de money you owe or someday soon your wife is widow.' Dat is de exact words me hear. And den of course de prosecutor bring in more witnesses, de ones who actually saw—"

"Saw what?"

"De violence dat takes place last night at Winnie's, a dispute breaking out among de customers and dey do a lot of damage, dey smash bottles and bust up de tables and chairs and many of de men are badly hurt. A gentlemon who was dere, he tell me about it. He say de gentlemen who later died in de alley was murdered by dis killer, who at first tried to knock he brains out wid table leg, and den try to get he with a chair aimed at he head, and later pull a knife and throw it but it miss. So den dis killer he leave Winnie's Place and he wait outside in de alley. You see, now he have no knife, he need other instrument. So he use broken bottle. Dey tell me it caused by broken bottle inserted in de victim's throat. Dey find de pieces of glass in he flesh so dey know it broken bottle. Of course, dis killer he not want dem to find de bottle, it would show he fingerprints, so dey assume he hide it somewhere. But dat no matter, dey not need de bottle for evidence. De evidence dey have is witnesses. Dere many witnesses and dey will tell all dat needs to be told. De jury will be out maybe two minutes, maybe three, no longer dan dat, it is safe to wager."

The taxi was making a turn off Duke, coming onto Barry Street and heading east.

"You still wish to go to Winnie's Place?" the driver asked.

"Yes," Bevan said. He said it emphatically.

"Very well, Mr. Captain. But you cause me to wonder. Me cannot understand why you insist to go to dat house."

Bevan didn't reply. He was thinking, It's easy to understand. It's the old fable of the demon slayer, pulled by the tide of whatever the hell it is that takes him back to the scene of the slaying.

Chapter Nine

You knew it all the time, he thought. You knew you'd come back here to see it again, to live through it again. He was standing in the sun-splashed, heat-drenched alley outside Winnie's Place, looking down at the dark-gray soil that showed through the broken paving. He noticed there were no garbage cans or tin cans or other rubbish in the area, and he knew it had all been cleared away during the early-morning search for the murder weapon. But they won't need that, he said to himself.

They certainly won't need that. As the taxi driver puts it, they've established the motive and they have witnesses who'll point their fingers at the accused and that'll do it, that'll finish him.

Well, now. What about that?

What are you going to do about it? You going to stand around and let it happen?

I think the only move is, we go to the police and let them know the truth. Yes, I think that's what we'll do.

Because it's the right thing to do? The fair thing to do? Or because you're primarily interested in being classified as a law-abiding individual?

No, it isn't that. It isn't any of that.

It's simply and solely because you have nothing to lose. You just don't give a damn. The most they can do is stretch your neck with a rope, and that's as good an exit as any. The thing is, you've been playing around with the idea of making an exit, so if they string you up they'll just be sparing you the effort.

All right, then. Forward, march. Let's see now, our friend the taxi driver gave us the location; he said police headquarters are on Queen Street. Very good, and what we do now is follow Barry to the first intersection and turn north toward Queen.

But he didn't move.

Well, he asked himself. What's the delay?

But there's really no hurry, not in terms of hours, anyway. If you want to, you can stand here for hours and shove it around, wrestle with it.

That's what it amounts to, a wrestling match. You're sitting at ringside and watching them going at it. In black tights we have Masked Demon, otherwise known as the ruined soul, he wants to end it all. In white tights, giving away a lot of weight and very definitely the underdog, an accumulation of living tissue that wants to remain alive. He's a slippery customer, that one in white tights. He slides out of those holds like an eel. But sooner or later he'll weaken, I'm willing to give odds on that. Let's make it seven to one.

Or maybe not. Better make it even money. Better yet, let's quit this clowning and get down to business. The business at hand is the clear-cut issue of going to the local gendarmes or not going to the local gendarmes. Let's assume you go to them and tell them you did it. You'll be saying you did it to protect yourself from an armed robber. You'll say he had a blackjack.

And of course they'll come right back at you with

what you know already, that they didn't find any blackjack. So that brings us to Mr. Nathan Joyner. You'll be forced to tell them of the deal you made with Joyner, although I don't think that'll work. I'm quite sure it won't work. If they call in Joyner they won't get anything from him. He'll make a flat denial, and he'd be foolish if he didn't. He'd be very foolish to let himself wide open for a charge of blackmail that would send him up for two years or three or maybe more. I think we can agree it's no use mentioning our chum Nathan.

That makes the blackjack factor somewhat awkward. All right, let's shelve that for a moment. Next item on the list, the broken bottle. They'll want to know what you did with it. Again the answer is Nathan, and that means there's no answer. You'll just sit there and stare at them stupidly.

At this point it begins to get stuffy in the room where they're asking the questions. So many questions, and when you try to answer, the words just won't come.

But they won't rush you. They'll be very considerate and very polite. It isn't as though you're some hoodlum they've picked up. You're a respectable American citizen, a first-class tourist staying at the fashionable Laurel Rock Hotel. So that cancels out the rough stuff. And yet I'd much prefer the rough stuff to the politeness. It's the politeness that makes you feel you're being slowly smothered. You swallow hard, and one of them picks up a pencil and makes a note of that.

And another leans forward with his hands flat on

the desk, smiling ever so politely as he asks, Why did you run away?

You fled from the scene, Mr. Bevan. We're interested in knowing why.

It—it isn't easy to explain.

What do you mean by that?

No answer.

Had you been drinking?

Yes.

Were you intoxicated?

I'm not sure.

You mean you can't remember?

I guess that's it.

How did you get back to the hotel?

I walked.

Then you weren't very drunk, Mr. Bevan. You weren't too drunk to know where you were going. It's quite evident you were capable of making a decision. You decided to get away from there as quickly as possible and return to the hotel. Am I correct in that assumption?

Yes.

When you entered the Laurel Rock, did anyone see you come in?

No.

But someone must have seen you. There are always employees in the lobby. The desk clerk has a clear view of the front entrance. Or perhaps you didn't use the front entrance?

May I have a drink of water?

Certainly. I think I'll have one myself. It's terribly

hot in here, isn't it? We ought to have a fan going. But the fans have been sent away for repairs. Oh, well, that's how it goes. Tell me, Mr. Bevan—which entrance did you use?

Side entrance.

Your room is on what floor?

Third.

Did anyone see you going up to your room?

No.

Not even the elevator operator?

I didn't use the elevator.

Why not?

No answer.

Why did you use the side entrance? Why did you use the stairway instead of the elevator?

No answer.

Perhaps I can provide the answer, Mr. Bevan. You wanted to avoid being seen. Isn't that true?

I don't know what you're getting at.

That's a nice suit you're wearing, Mr. Bevan. Is it the same suit you wore last night?

No.

Could I see the suit you wore last night? I mean, if we went to the hotel, would you show it to me?

No answer.

You discarded that suit, didn't you? It was stained with blood and you were extremely anxious to get rid of it.

The suit was ruined. It was a mess and I just threw it away, that's all.

But you also got rid of the broken bottle. What about that?

No answer.

Another thing, Mr. Bevan. You stated the man was armed with a blackjack. When I told you there was no blackjack, and no evidence to indicate he had such a weapon, you failed to provide an explanation. Can you explain it now?

No answer.

What is it, Mr. Bevan? Why can't you reply to these questions? I'm sure you'd feel a lot better if you let it all out and told me the truth.

All right, I'll say it again. He was trying to rob me.

And you merely tried to defend yourself. But that makes it all the more puzzling. You claim what you did was fully justifiable. But your behavior following the incident fails to support that claim. If you'll pardon my putting it bluntly, each and every move you made was the act of a fugitive.

Now look, I wasn't dragged in here. I came here voluntarily.

And we appreciate that, Mr. Bevan. It's certainly a point in your favor. Unfortunately, it doesn't hold up for long. It becomes another segment that fits the pattern.

What pattern?

The pattern of your strategy.

I don't know what you mean.

Yes, you do, Mr. Bevan. You know precisely what I mean.

I've told you—

What you told me wasn't the truth. Not the whole truth. There's a missing element involved here. It's more a question of motivation than anything else. Do you care to help me out on that?

No answer.

All right, Mr. Bevan. That's all for now.

So later they try again, but of course you won't answer. You won't read it off to them from the billboard you saw in your sleep, the words in big black letters, "He went out to spill some blood and spilled it, that's all." It's a plain statement that anyone can understand; it needs no analyzing or theorizing or a careful study of my brain. These things happen every day. All you need to do is pick up any paper and there it is on the front page. Man Slain by Unknown Assailant. They pick up a number of suspects and all of them have alibis except one creepy-looking bird who has trouble answering the questions and finally gives a shrug and says, "All right, boys, you got me." But when they ask him if he knew the victim he says no, he never saw the man before in his life. So then they ask him why he did it and he says he just felt like doing it to someone, he happened to be in that kind of mood. They check on him and find out he works in an office where the supervisor makes it miserable for him, has been doing it for years, all of it piling up in him like a stack of fire-crackers just waiting for that one tiny spark to set them off. Or one time I remember it was a man who used a sledge hammer, waiting behind a parked truck for the

first person that came along. It came out in the court-
room he'd been having a twenty-year feud with his
father-in-law, with the old man making all the noise
and dishing it out, or rather slamming it down on his
head with the force of a sledge hammer. So when he
had to take it out on someone it couldn't be an ordinary hammer or a length of lead pipe; it had to be a big
heavy tool he'd be wielding with both hands.

Well, you were provoked into doing it. But you
were itching to be provoked, and that's the size of it,
mister. And while we're at it, we can narrow it down to
the essential fact that you wanted his blackjack to
smash the bottle, you wanted jagged glass to enter his
throat.

But is that a fact? Is that really a fact?

The answer is either yes or no; there's no in-
between. And at this particular point there's a decided
lack of reasons to say no, and there's every reason to
say yes.

And that's it. Mr. Investigator. That's the missing
element you wanted me to provide. Now that you
have it, you can release the man you picked up this
morning, and you can throw me in a cell without fear
of any repercussions from the American Consulate.
You'll simply tell them you have the slayer in custody
and the slayer has made a confession that clarifies the
motive. You'll tell them it was premeditated, based on
the technical factor of an urge to destroy. The intent is
clearly indicated by the cause of the victim's death, the
broken bottle aimed at a vital spot, entering the throat

and severing the jugular vein. Are there any further questions?

I don't think so. Unless it's the question that first came up, the question of whether or not you're ready and willing to hang.

You want them to hang you?

No. Not really. If they do that, I'll miss out on a lot of drinking. And I enjoy drinking. It's the only enjoyment there is, but it's a very pleasant thing and I'd like to stay with it.

What you mean is you want to remain alive.

More or less.

Then you won't go to Queen Street? You won't give yourself up?

I'm going into Winnie's Place and get a drink.

Just a moment.

Sorry, mister. I'm in a hurry.

But listen. The man they arrested, he's innocent. You know he's innocent. What about that?

I can't talk to you now. I'm awfully thirsty.

You won't try to help him?

Oh, leave me alone. For Christ's sake, leave me alone. And then he was moving quickly, convulsively. He went down the alley to the side door of Winnie's Place, grabbed at the knob like someone overboard grabbing at a life buoy. The door was on loose hinges and it made a loud creaking sound as he threw it open. He let it stay open as he stumbled in, tripping over a crumbled cardboard box, then tripping again as he collided with an overturned chair with two of its legs

missing. There were several overturned chairs, most
of them needing repair, and some of the tables were in
similar condition. There was a lot of broken glass on
the floor, and the bar itself was badly splintered. He
came up to it and leaned on it, and it sagged under his
weight. Then one of the boards fell away from the
frontal side, and as it went down it narrowly missed a
frantic mouse scurrying out from underneath the bar.
He heard the thin squeak and turned his head to
watch the mouse going pell-mell across the littered
floor, cutely by-passing the sprawled legs of Winnie,
who sat on a toolbox staring dismally at nothing at all.
Her arms dangled limply and in one hand she held a
screwdriver. The fingers of her other hand were
wrapped loosely and futilely around a small pot of
glue. At her feet there were scattered nails and screws
of various sizes, a pair of rusty pliers, and a small hack-
saw with its blade twisted out of shape.

As Bevan gazed at her, she gave a sigh and let go of
the glue pot. It rolled along the floor and the glue
came out in a slow thick flood. She watched the glue
pouring out of the overturned pot, her mouth gradually
forming a somewhat contented smile. Then carefully
she aimed the screwdriver at the stream of glue,
pitching it overhanded and sending it into the thick
amber stream. She looked at her empty hands, clapped
her palms to make an emphatic sound of finality, and
said, "Dat settles dat."

"Sell me a drink," Bevan said.

She didn't look up. It was as though she hadn't

heard. Again she spoke aloud to herself. "De tools are not useful when dere is no ability to use them."

"That makes sense," Bevan remarked. "But it doesn't get me a drink. I came here to get a drink."

She looked at him, then looked past him and said, "You got a box of matches?"

"Matches? For what?"

"To burn up dis place."

"You serious?"

"Give me de matches and I demonstrate."

He glanced around the room with its wrecked tables and chairs, with its walls showing wide holes where the plaster had given way. Winnie was saying, "Dey break up dis place for the last time. What dey do here last night was de end of it. Dey make de damage once too often."

"Is that how you feel about it?"

"Dat is precisely how I feel about it."

"Then we both need a bracer."

Winnie let that slide. She was gazing at the glue spilled on the floor. "Look at dis mess," she said. "Look at what dey do to my establishment."

"Come on, let's have that bracer. You open up a bottle and we'll get ourselves braced and have a party."

"Dis not de time for a party."

"It's the perfect time," he said. "I can't think of a better time for filling the glasses and having a party."

She smiled at him. It was a contemplative smile, very dry and somewhat twisted. She said, "You wish to make dis a festive occasion?"

"Sure." He grinned at her. "You set up the glasses and we'll commence the festivities."

"To celebrate what?" She made a slow gesture to indicate the smashed furniture and ripped walls and littered floor. "You see any reason to celebrate?"

"I'll find a reason. I'm always finding reasons to celebrate."

Winnie lifted herself from the toolbox. She moved slowly to the splintered bar and went behind it, ducking under it and coming up with an unopened bottle of rum. Then she searched for glasses and couldn't find any that weren't broken. She walked out of the room and came back with a tin cup and a water glass. Bevan was busy with the task of uncapping the bottle.

When he got it opened he poured the rum into the clean water glass and the somewhat battered tin cup. Winnie reached mechanically toward the tin cup and the American tourist pulled it way from her and offered her the water glass.

"I drink from de cup," she said. "De cup is all right for me."

But she didn't get the point across. He wasn't paying attention. He had the tin cup to his lips and was taking a long gulp of rum.

She looked at the water glass set before her, and made no move to take it. She said, "You enjoying dis party?"

"Very much." He grinned at her. "It's a swell party."

"It would be nicer if I could provide entertainment."

"Like a floor show?"

"Yes," she said. "Wid much noise. Much activity. Like you see here last night."

He took another gulp of rum. He didn't say anything.

"I remember you from last night," Winnie said. "You de same mon. De same clean-face, clean-shirt tourist who come here to view de exhibit."

"Exhibit?"

"Yes, mon. De comical exhibit of de comical people. I hope you were pleased wid de performance."

He wasn't grinning now. He said very quietly, "You're dialing the wrong number."

She looked at the money he'd placed on the bar. She said, "Put it back in your pocket. De bottle is my treat."

He shrugged. "You're the boss."

Then he was returning the bills to the wallet, putting the wallet in his pocket. Winnie was saying, "You call me de boss. But you know I am not de boss. At de hotel where you stay I would be cleaning de toilets."

"Oh, cut it out," he said. "You're spoiling the party."

"You are right. I should not spoil de party for you. I should do my best to provide de frolic for de tourist mon. Perhaps you would like me to dance?"

She came out from behind the bar and simulated a dancing pose. He looked at her shapeless body, which showed all the strain and weariness of fifty-odd years in the sugar fields and the tobacco factories, the labor-hardened ridges engraved deeply in the dark skin. Her blemished and almost chinless face was creased in a wide smile of pretended gaiety, and he saw it was an imitation of the "gay, colorful native women" as they danced in the pages of the travel folders.

She said, "De tourist mon, he like to see de shoulders shake, de feet doing de meringue, de beguine, de calypso. And de native woman she half naked or entirely naked, like she supposed to be for benefit of tourist mon. He clap hands to make her dance faster. And faster yet. And still faster. He take de coins from his pocket and pitch de silver onto de floor. 'Shake it, girlie,' he shout at her, and so she shakes it wid all her might, in accordance wid de wishes of de clean-face tourist. You see, she need dese coins. In de house her babies are sick, dey require medicine. Or in dis particular case it is younger brother who is in trouble and requires a lawyer."

Something very cold hit him in the eyes. Then it burned white-hot. And then it was cold again.

He heard her saying, "Dere is no money for a lawyer. And even if dere was, it would be money thrown away. Because no lawyer can save him. Nothing can save him."

The dancing pose had been abandoned. Now it was a stoop-shouldered shuffle that took her back behind the bar.

She lifted the glass of rum and said, "You drink a toast wid me, mon?"

He nodded. It was a slow nod, somewhat mechanical.

She said, "We drink to dis younger brother of mine.

Last night he cut de mon in de throat and de mon he
die. It happen out dere in de alley. Dis morning de
police catch my brother and so now we drink to he and
wish he a pleasant trip to de gallows."

The rum never reached her mouth. The glass fell
out of her hand and the rum spilled over the bar. Then
her head was down, her hands covering her face.

Chapter Ten

He wondered what he could say to her. It seemed rather pointless to say anything, or do anything. If he patted her shoulder consolingly she wouldn't even feel it, so perhaps the only move was to pour more rum into the tin cup and drink it down and then drink some more.

The tin cup was filled and emptied and refilled. It went on like that for a while, the rum sliding down very smoothly, the vapors of it floating up to his brain and swirling slowly, amounting to a whirlpool that beckoned him, telling him it was so pleasant down there, far away from everything. Yet as he descended into the amber fog of rum-induced nothingness, he saw Winnie raising her head, gazing past him at the ruin of her establishment.

He looked at her eyes, and he knew she was seeing beyond the smashed chairs and tables and battered walls. She was seeing the wreckage of something that couldn't be repaired.

So then he realized why she'd given up trying with the pot of glue and the screwdriver and the other tools. The glue and the tools had nothing to do with the broken wood. It didn't need much thinking to understand that. It came to him from her eyes, which were saying, What is de use? Why attempt to fix what cannot be fixed?

He knew she meant the younger brother, and even before she said it aloud he sensed the countless efforts she'd made to correct the wayward child who became a wayward youth and then a wayward man.

She was saying, "Dat Eustace, he give me grief from de time when we very young and my parents die. It just Eustace and me, and I do what I can to take care of he. I try to teach he what is right, but he no listen. He run out in de street and make de mischief. Den later he begin to steal I beat he on head wid stick. I say, 'You have de devil in you, boy. I knock he out of you. It is devil I hit, not you.' But Eustace, he have very hard head. He only laugh and say, 'For devil you need bigger stick. Something heavy to make he feel it. Like cricket bat.' So one time he come home wid turtles he steal from fish stall in de Coronation Market, and I hit he wid cricket bat. Yes, I certainly give it to he dat time. He go to hospital wid what dey tell me is concussion of de brain. But does dat send de devil away? No, it only put devil in deeper. When Eustace come out of the hospital he badder dan ever.

"Come de day when he steal one time too many and dey catch he. Dey put he in de school for de bad ones. But dat only make it worse. He out less dan week when dey put he in again. Den out and den in again. Out and in, out and in. And what is to be done? It is a question I ask myself so many nights in de bed when I weep on de pillow, because even if he is bad, de fact remain he my brother and de devil is eating he up.

"When he nineteen he past de age for de correction school and when dey catch he stealing on de docks dey send he to prison. I say to myself, Maybe now he will learn. But only things he learn in prison is more tricks and capers. In prison de art of wrongdoing has many professors and de pupils are willing and anxious to be taught. He twenty-three when he out and twenty-four when he in again. Next time dey let he out he twenty-nine, and he go back in when he thirty-one. Dere is occasion when I had some money saved from working in de tobacco factory, and I visit de prison and I say to Eustace, 'I soon have money enough to start a business, to buy a license and sell drinks. When dey let you out, you come and work dere wid me.' And Eustace say, 'Dat is fine idea, Winnie. I like dat very much. You and me, we be in business together, we sell much rum and make much money. I buy nice clothes and be respectable mon.' So den when he is thirty-six he out of prison and I obtain de license to sell de alcohol beverages. De first night when we are open for business my brother Eustace he go out wid two men and dey rob a store on King Street."

Bevan reached for the bottle and the water glass. He poured rum into the glass and offered it to Winnie. She shook her head, but he nodded coaxingly. She took the glass and drank the rum, all of it, holding the glass pressed tightly against her mouth with her head thrown far back. Then she was looking at the empty glass as she extended it slowly for a refill.

He filled it, and also filled the tin cup. Now the bottle was three-quarters empty. For a while they stood there drinking and not saying anything. They finished the bottle and started another. He said he was paying for the second bottle. Winnie said no, whatever they drank was her treat. He insisted on paying and it became an argument, their drink-thickened voices mixing in a swirl of incoherent phrases that went round and round and didn't get anywhere. But finally she gave in, and he put the money on the bar. They grinned at each other, then began to work diligently on the second bottle.

But gradually the grin went away from her face. The rum tried to hold it there and couldn't hold it and she was talking again about her brother. She said, "De last time he come out of prison it two years ago. He say to me, 'Winnie, I have learned my lesson. I make solemn promise.' I look at him and I say, 'You tell me dat so often, I am tired of hearing it.' But he say very seriously, 'I prove it to you, Winnie. You will see.' And when I tell he to bring he clothes here, he refuse so quietly, so much formality de way he say, 'I thank you, my sister. But I cannot accept your generosity. Always it is you who do de giving, who make de sacrifice for a worthless brother. But in my heart I am a mon and it is time now to demonstrate de truth of dat.' I watch as he walk away. He walk very straight, and de head it is up.

"De very next day he get job in garage. I tink to myself it is maybe good sign. De weeks pass and den de months and he keep working at de job. In de afternoons I walk past de garage and I see he working harder dan anyone else. In de meantime he get woman to live with, a nice clean woman he bring to me for my approval. From time to time she come to visit me, and she tell me she very pleased wid Eustace, he kind to her and treat her wid much courtesy and respect. He not run out at night, and go to bed early, and I see de brightness in her eyes dat means she happy wid her mon.

"Last year dey have child, a boy. And dis year twin girls. In de garage Eustace get raise in salary and dey move to larger rooms. Dey so contented wid each other and de children and at night when I say prayers I give thanks to de Lord.

"But it could not last. I should have known it could not last. De garage it close down and Eustace he out of work. De times are bad and he cannot find employment. I tell he to come and work here, I need someone here to help me. He say, 'Help you wid what? Where are de customers?' De answer, of course, is dere are no customers when de condition of un-employment is prevailing in Kingston. Also, it is time when dere are no ships in de harbor. When dat happens, it is matter dat requires much thought and planning. When de belly is getting empty one must use de brains.

"Eustace, he use he brains to gamble. He take what few coins he have, he go out at night and flip de dice, deal de cards. Many times he win, only a few times he lose. He win because he clever wid dice and cards. But not cheater. Decidedly not cheater. He win dat money honestly to feed children and woman. But even so dere no excuse for what he do last night. I try to look for excuse and find none. In de alley he pounce on de mon, he take de mon's life. And for what reason?

"Reason is gambling debt. De mon owe de money

and refuse to pay. De sum involved is grand total of one pound, two shillings."

Bevan was pouring more rum into the tin cup and the water glass.

"One pound, two shillings," Winnie said.

She gulped the rum. But now it was too much rum and it really hit her and she started to laugh.

"A piece of paper and two coins," she said, laughing loudly, rackingly.

"It wasn't that," he said.

But she didn't hear. Her laughter covered it.

"I said it wasn't that."

It didn't get through; the laughter was too loud.

Winnie was saying, "We announce de list of casualties. De mon who died in de alley, he got woman and five small children. We add dat number to four in family of mon who will die for deed. Six and four is—"

"Listen, lady. Listen to me—"

"—is nine? No, is ten. Dat is correct, dere ten of dem. Dere eight children and two mothers. And when dey visit de graves of de fathers—"

"But listen—"

"Dey will look at de graves, dey will remember why it happened. A gambling debt, de sum amounting to one pound, two shillings."

And she laughed again, more loudly now. The laughter was choking her. But all at once she stopped laughing and looked at him. She saw his eyes focused on the open door.

She turned her head to see what was in the doorway. There was nothing in the doorway, just the sunlight coming in, the slanting ribbons of bright yellow with billions of dust particles floating downward through the stream of light. Then again she looked at his face, watching his eyes, which were aimed level at the doorway, as though he saw something or someone coming in very slowly, coming toward him.

He took a backward step, then another, and another.

But that was all. Because there was no getting away from it. He stood waiting, his lips gradually curving in a twisted grin, his rum-glazed eyes saying, I'm ready now.

His arm moved out just a little, as though a hand had fallen on his wrist and were leading him toward the door. He was going toward the door and Winnie was saying, "What is it, mon? Why you leaving?"

"The party's over," he said.

She gaped at him as he walked out.

Chapter Eleven

He walked in a straight path down the alley to Barry Street, then along Barry to the first corner that allowed him to turn north, toward Queen. Queen Street was crowded and his path was blocked by groups of people chattering and laughing, or engaged in various business transactions that consisted mostly of loud dispute and vigorous gestures of negation. But he saw none of it, heard none of it. He drifted through it in a trance-like manner that they noticed as they saw him coming. It caused them to step aside and make way for him, staring at him as he passed, then staring at one another in the sudden stillness induced by wide-eyed wonder.

"Dat mon, he move like sleepwalker," one said.

"Or hypnotized," another commented. "He look hypnotized."

"You both wrong," a third one said. "Dat mon, he drink too much."

"But look how straight he walk," the first one said. "He walk too straight to be drunk."

"I insist de mon is drunk," the other said. "He do not know where he go. I will make wager—"

"You would lose," the first one said. "Dat mon, he know precisely where he go."

They stood there watching the neatly attired tourist, who had crossed to the other side of Queen Street and was headed toward the entrance of police headquarters.

He told it to three dark-skinned policemen, facing them where they stood just inside the entrance. They listened impassively, and then one of them said, "Come with me, sir," and took him across the anteroom to a desk where a very fat police sergeant sat with folded arms, glaring at two skinny women who wore excessive lipstick and rouge and powder. The sergeant's skin was coal black, but somehow it reflected a vermilion tint, a sulphurous glow that was more the heat of anger than the heat of the day. The sergeant was saying to the women, "Last time I let you off with warning. But dis time—"

The policeman interrupted, moving in close to the sergeant and whispering in his ear. The sergeant's mouth opened very slowly, became wide, and stayed that way as the policeman went on whispering. A large blue-winged fly settled on the sergeant's nose, but he made no move to brush it away. Finally the policeman stepped back and waited for a comment. There was no comment. The sergeant just sat there and let the fly stay on his nose as he gaped at the American tourist, who stood grinning.

Then the fly went away. It flew around in wide circles above the sergeant's head. Bevan watched it, the grin saying, How is it up there? and the fly replying, It's simply grand, provided you have wings. Bevan lost the grin for a moment. He got it back as one of the skinny women forgot where she was and winked at him. He winked back. Then the woman was smiling invitingly and trying to flaunt her bony hip, but the policeman came in close and loomed above her, his pointed finger moving like a needle toward her forehead. So her hip went back into place and she gave a little shrug that told the law it had won the round and she was passing up this customer. The sergeant nodded to the policeman, who wrapped his large hands around the wrists of the women and led them away. Then the sergeant said to Bevan, "I cannot believe what de policeman tells me. Perhaps you can clarify?"

So then he told it to the sergeant. The sergeant took out a handkerchief and mopped his sweating face as he got up from the desk. "This way, sir." He led Bevan toward a corridor. They went down the corridor to a door marked "Lieutenants."

He told it to a lieutenant, and presently he was telling it to several lieutenants. They didn't know what to do with it, and decided it was something that needed the captain. They took him into the office of the captain, who subsequently called in another captain. There was some whispered discussion between the captains, and finally they agreed they couldn't handle this, the only thing to do was bring it to the inspector.

The inspector's name was Archinroy and he was the product of mixed races several generations back. His skin was a yellow-gray, some of the yellow resulting from a liver condition, but most of it due to the great-great-grandmother who had been a native of Sumatra and had married the British heir to a rubber plantation.

As a result of the marriage, the heir was disinherited and didn't mind it too much. Gradually he lost his Oxford accent and developed a taste for rice and dried fish. They had seven children and one of the sons went to Africa, where he married a Nigerian girl who gave him three black children, one of them an ambitious boy who went to England and studied law and married a mulatto girl who had come over from British Honduras. Their only child was a son, who also wanted to be a lawyer, but a war intervened and he got hit during the First Battle of the Marne. A few months later, his young widow gave birth to an undersized boy with slightly slanted eyes and a yellow-gray skin.

Inspector Archinroy retained the slightly slanted eyes through all the years of growing up in the Limehouse section of London, where at first he went in for petty thievery, his eyes getting narrower as he learned all the tricks. Later, when he decided to become a policeman, his former associates tried to do away with him, but his slanted narrow eyes were both telescopic and microscopic, and he saw through every move they made. He foxed them right and left and achieved quite a reputation for making arrests and making the charges stick. Of course, he was promoted, promoted again and then again, the promotions continuing through fourteen years in New Scotland Yard. What ultimately removed him from New Scotland Yard was the need for high-grade law-enforcement officials in certain of the crown colonies where criminal activity had got out of hand. It was mostly homicide,

and Archinroy's specialty was the interrogation of
suspects, playing with them as though at a game of
billiards, fooling them into thinking they were scoring
with their answers, then quietly and almost caressingly
touching them with the one question that shattered all
the alibis, sending them to the rope or the prison
where they'd stay for the rest of their lives. He did a
lot of that in Georgetown, British Guiana, and more
of it in San Fernando, Trinidad, where outbreaks of
homicide came periodically, like epidemics. He remained in Trinidad for eleven years, and then was
assigned to Kingston, Jamaica. They felt his special
talent was badly needed in Kingston. The police were
making arrests but not getting convictions, and the
situation required someone who could obtain quick
confessions so that the newspapers could announce
the date of the hangings, thus telling Kingstonians it
was no longer easy to get away with homicide. At that
time there was considerable homicide in Kingston.

Now he'd been in Kingston six years. He was fifty-
six and should have looked at least ten years older,
considering the type of work he did, but actually he
looked twenty years younger. The only lines on his
face were a few scars. Two were knife scars and one
was from the thumbnail of a woman who had drowned
her several children and later went berserk during the
questioning. Things like that should have put some
gray in his hair, or removed a portion of his hair. But
there was no gray hair and he had all of it, parting it
close to the middle, brushing it flat across to the tem-
ples, oiling it lightly so it was a shiny black, but not too

shiny. The same applied to his shoes. His shoes were
never excessively shined. It appeared he knew just
when to stop using the rubbing cloth. With his meals
and with his use of tobacco, too, the degree of moder-
ation never changed. He seemed to use some invisible
measuring device that told him exactly where and
when to stop.

He was only five-six and weighed around 130, but he
didn't look small as he sat there at the desk, his slanted
narrow eyes shooting out a yellow gleam that seemed to
surround him and magnify him, so that whatever it was
that came from his eyes, it made him appear much
taller than five-six, much heavier than 130.

He said to Bevan, "Is that all of it?"

"Yes," Bevan said.

"Are you quite sure?"

Bevan shrugged. "Why dig for more? I've given you
all you need."

"Possibly," Archinroy murmured. But then he did
something that was either a negative gesture or a
meaningless gesture or an attempt to tighten the gears
of his mind. He put his hands flat on the top of his
head and pressed hard.

They were alone in the room. It was a small office
furnished with a few chairs facing the desk, a couple of
filing cabinets, and a floor-model electric fan that
revolved very fast but made only a little noise. This
was a fine electric fan and it cooled the room to just
the right degree. Or maybe it isn't the fan, Bevan
thought. Maybe the coolness is coming from the
inspector.

He's certainly a cool one, this inspector. Oh, well, they're supposed to be cool. That's their stock in trade. But this one is really a cucumber, a perfect model for an advertisement featuring light-weave suits. But what about his sweat glands? Doesn't he have any sweat glands? The others were all sweating, the captains and the lieutenants and especially that fat sergeant. I sure had them sweating. I'll bet they never heard anything like that. This one ought to be sweating, too. He's top turkey here and it's up to him to make the decision, but look at the coolness of him. Except for the way his hands are pressing on his head, as though he's got a migraine headache or something. Yet his face is strictly zero, nothing moving, nothing showing. It's as though he were alone in here, taking a nap with his eyes open.

But then Archinroy came out of it, whatever it was. He lowered his hands to the desk, his fingertips lightly playing on the blotter pad. He did that for several moments, watching the play of his fingers, as though rehearsing something he intended to perform on a piano. Finally he looked up at Bevan and said, "Let's try it again."

"You mean you want me to change it?"

"Not unless it needs changing."

"What do you mean by that?"

"It might need changing," Archinroy said. "If you think about it—"

"There's nothing to think about. I've told you what happened, how it happened, and why it happened. I've given a full confession, and if you want me to put it on paper and sign it, I'll be glad to do so."

"Why?"

Bevan winced. Then he grinned at the inspector. He said, "Is that a teaser?"

"It could be," Archinroy murmured. "Depends on the way you take it."

"It doesn't worry me." He sent the grin past the inspector. He wasn't talking to the inspector as he said, "Nothing worries me. I'm worryproof."

"What's that again?"

"Worryproof," Bevan said. He looked at the inspector. "It's something new on the market. It's a special treatment you can give yourself at home. Very easy to take, once you have the knack. There's really nothing to it."

"Perhaps I'll try it sometime," Archinroy said. Again his fingers hit the invisible piano keys. His eyes were focused on the blotter pad as he said, "I want you to repeat your confession."

"All right." Bevan shrugged. "But I wish we had a tape recorder. I'm getting tired of all these encores."

Archinroy leaned back in the chair. "Ready?"

"For anything," Bevan said. Then again he was gazing past the Inspector. He was talking to an audience far beyond the Inspector as he said, "I'm a guest at the Laurel Rock Hotel. Yesterday afternoon I went out for a stroll. Not to see the sights, not to get exercise. It was more like going out on an assignment, although I wasn't quite sure where I was headed. I don't know how far I walked or where I went, although I remember turning a lot of corners and it must have been a very long walk.

"Then when it was dark I happened to be on Barry Street, and I went into this house called Winnie's Place. I sat down at a table and had some rum. It was awfully good rum and I bought some more. And then more. I was having a swell time sitting there drinking the rum when there was some disagreement among the other customers and they began slamming each other around and throwing things. I wanted more rum, but there was so much activity and no one around to serve me, so I decided to get out of there and go some other place where I could buy more rum. But actually I didn't want the rum.

"Actually I wanted blood."

He was repeating it almost word for word, as he'd told it to the sergeant and the lieutenants and the captains, as he'd told it previously to the Inspector.

"I wanted blood," Bevan went on. "I wanted to see it spilled and I was hoping for a chance to hit at something. So then in the alley outside Winnie's Place I hear this sound and I turn around and there he is. I picked up a bottle and made a pass at him. The bottle breaks and I guess you know how it is when you've got hold of a broken bottle and you're in the mood to use it on something to see the blood come out. You have a grudge against the universe for a number of reasons and you've got to take it out on some living thing. Reason I'm putting it this way, I want you to know I knew what I was doing when I jabbed that broken bottle in his throat."

"And then what?" the Inspector murmured.

"Then I ran away," Bevan said. He shrugged and

added, "Today I got to thinking about it, and I went to Winnie's Place for another look at that alley. You know how it is, the old routine, we're always pulled back to the scene of the party. And later I'm sharing a bottle with Winnie and she tells me you've arrested her brother."

"Is that your reason for coming here? To protect her brother?"

"I came here to tell you the truth."

"Then tell it." The Inspector's narrow eyes became narrower. "What really happened?"

"Let's leave it the way it is. Don't try to twist it. There's no way to twist it."

"I suppose not," Archinroy said aloud to himself. And then, to Bevan, "You really believe what you're saying. If I tried to contradict, I'd be talking to the wall. You're sitting there but actually you're not there. There's no use in trying further questions."

"Why not? I'm willing to answer."

Archinroy smiled. It was a kindly smile. There was a tinge of pity in it. He said, "All right, let's give it a test. Let's see if we can bring it onto solid ground. To begin with, what happened to the broken bottle?"

Bevan didn't answer.

Archinroy leaned back in his chair and waited.

Bevan grinned at him and then aimed the grin at the floor.

The Inspector went on smiling kindly, pityingly. Now he was looking down at the blotter pad as he said, "Tell me something, Mr. Bevan. Have you ever had treatment?"

"Treatment? For what?"

"Emotional disturbance."

Bevan blinked several times. "Well—" He rubbed his fingers hard across his forehead. "Well, yes. I've been to a neurologist."

"Did he diagnose your condition?"

"He said— Oh, the hell with what he said."

Archinroy went on looking down at the blotter pad. "We have some good ones here in Kingston. I can recommend—"

"Save it." He felt the sickly grimace coming onto his face and there was nothing he could do to get it off. The words squeezed through his clenched teeth. "Don't get cute with me. You can shoot the questions, but don't get cute."

The Inspector spoke quietly. "There are no further questions."

"Then pick up the phone and call them in. Tell them to put the cuffs on me and lock me up."

Archinroy's smile widened just a little. "You'd like that, wouldn't you?"

Bevan didn't reply.

"You'd like that very much," Archinroy said. "But I'm afraid we can't accommodate you."

"Now look—"

"I'm not accepting your confession," Archinroy interrupted.

Bevan blinked again. The sickly grimace became tighter, deeper. He heard a groan and wondered if it came from his own lips.

The Inspector said, "Do you wish to leave now?"

Bevan stared at the desktop. He saw the green blotter pad and there were no papers on it, just the inkwell and the pen arranged neatly to one side. He said, "You didn't even bother to write it down."

"Because you've given me nothing that I can use." The Inspector spoke softly, gently. "My usual practice is to make notes, but only when I hear something relevant and pertinent, something that will make sense when it reaches the courtroom."

"Thanks," Bevan said. "Thanks a lot."

Archinroy was quiet for some moments. He seemed to be trying to find the right words, the words that wouldn't be too blunt, that wouldn't hit too hard. Finally he said, "You're a confused man. Terribly confused, and certainly not responsible for your statements. It's a nervous condition known as—"

"They all want to be doctors," Bevan cut in.

"I was saying—"

"You were saying nothing," he cut in again. "My nervous condition. What do you know about my nervous condition?"

Archinroy picked up the fountain pen and played it between his fingers. "I've come across many similar cases. After all, I've been working in this field for a long time. Some thirty-six years, to be exact."

"Maybe you're pooped and you need a rest."

"Hardly," the Inspector said. "There's nothing wrong with my metabolism. The only trouble I have is a liver ailment, a gunshot wound that didn't heal properly. But I'm sure it hasn't affected the top floor." He tapped the side of his head. "I'm sure the gears are all there

and fully capable of making decisions. In this case it's
no sale."

"But I did it. I'm telling you I did it."

"You didn't do anything except considerable drinking.
You had too much last night and today you were at it
again. It never helps, you know. What you need is a
first-rate specialist who can get you started on therapy,
at least keep you from walking into police stations and
making irrational statements."

Then it was ended. The Inspector was making a
polite but nonetheless definite gesture of dismissal.

Bevan lifted himself from the chair. He started to
say something and couldn't get it going. He was shaking
his head slowly as he walked out of the room.

Inspector Archinroy opened the desk drawer and took
out some papers that had to do with a case involving a
practitioner of Obeah, an old woman whose fake or
genuine witchcraft had caused three deaths among the
acquaintances of her clients. He glanced through the
papers and decided he had it wrapped up tightly
enough to obtain a conviction. Folding the papers and
putting them in an envelope, he got up from the desk
and carried the envelope across the room to the filing
cabinet. It had three drawers and he opened the top
drawer, which was labeled "C.C.," meaning "Cases
Closed." In the brain of the Inspector the "C.C." actually stood for "See? See?" which meant that these
cases were sufficiently closed so that they required no
further investigation. With a pencil he quickly scrawled
the old woman's first name and the initial of her last

name on the envelope, then dropped the envelope into the drawer. There was no alphabetical index in this drawer, and the envelope on which he had just written "Matilda B." rested loosely alongside an envelope on which was written "Eustace H."

Inspector Archinroy closed the drawer of the filing cabinet and went back to his desk.

Chapter Twelve

As Bevan came out of police headquarters, some children ran up to him and asked for pennies. He put his hand in his pocket, reaching for coins. Then he changed his mind and his hand went into the pocket where he kept his wallet. He took out the wallet, which contained some ninety dollars in American and British paper, and close to two hundred dollars in travelers' checks. There were seven children grouped around him and he gave each of them a pound note. They were unable to say anything, and they had difficulty breathing as they stood gaping at the money in their hands. A very old Jamaican came limping from a doorway and held out his hand and Bevan gave him a ten-dollar bill. Then more Jamaicans came forward and Bevan continued to hand out money until some policemen appeared and one of them barked, "You leave dis mon alone. Can't you see he is not well?"

So that broke it up. But later it happened again on Duke Street, where he distributed forty dollars among various men and women and children, whose ages ranged from seven to ninety. He was having a fine time, not from watching their faces as they received the money, only from seeing it going out of his hands, seeing the wallet getting thinner. What broke it up this time was an argument among the Jamaicans when one of them dropped a pound note and another picked it up and claimed possession. This resulted in considerable activity, the others taking sides and several of them using their feet as well as their hands. Bevan walked away from it, but some of the children followed him and he kept passing out the paper until there were no cash notes remaining.

Then later, on King Street, he was passing a bank when he saw some employees coming out and he went up to one of them and said he knew it was long past closing time but he'd be glad to pay for the extra service. So they went into the bank and the clerk took the traveler's checks from him and asked if he wanted the cash in American or British money. He said it didn't matter. The clerk gave it to him in British money. He gave the clerk the equivalent of some twenty dollars. The clerk said there must be some mistake. Of course, he was very grateful, but perhaps the gentleman failed to understand these were pound notes. But he wasn't staying to listen. The clerk went on trying to talk to him as he walked out of the bank.

He walked south on King, and at the intersection of King and Harbour he turned west. He had no idea where he was going. He was waiting for anyone at all to come up and ask for money. There were moments when it occurred to him that he had no logical reason for handing out money. That in itself was a satisfying thought; he wasn't interested in logical reasons. To do anything logically was too much of an effort, and when people followed that pattern they were only kidding themselves. Coming down to the core of it, this thing called logic or common sense or normal behavior or whatever you wanted to call it was nothing more than a blindfold that covered the inner eye. It kept people from seeing themselves, every goddamn one of them here in Kingston and in all of Jamaica, in all of the continent and the hemisphere and let's take it all the way and say both hemispheres. So if the question is asked, What's it amount to? the answer comes sliding out easily: It's just a merry-go-round that stops every now and then for some to get off and others to get on, and no matter how much you pay for your ticket, no matter how many brass rings you snatch, it's only a matter of time before your place is taken by the next customer emerging from some womb to start the ride. So in the final analysis, it's merely the process of being taken for a ride, and despite all the bright colors and the hurdy-gurdy music, despite the gleeful yells as the amusement machine goes round and round, the windup is a hole in the ground where the night crawlers get awfully hungry when it rains.

He didn't know it, but he was flat on his face in a muddy ditch that bordered a vacant lot off Harbour Street. He had stumbled into the lot, finally giving way to the quart and a half of rum he'd had at Winnie's, the alcohol he'd managed to carry with straight-spined balance all through the late afternoon and the fading daylight. But the rum had to hit him sooner or later, and as the sun fell into the Caribbean, the hundred-proof blaster moved in and hauled off, taking swings at him. In the darkness that came all too quickly he was falling into a sea much deeper than the Caribbean. So while he'd thought of the merry-go-round, he'd actually staggered in circles going away from Harbour Street and into the vacant lot. The lights of Harbour Street were within range of his vision, but he couldn't see them as street lamps and lighted windows; they added up to nothing more than a dim ribbon of yellow-green slime that curled and coiled all around him. His eyes were playing tricks on the brain that wanted to stop working and couldn't stop working. Perhaps it was his animal need for sleep that pushed him toward the ditch he couldn't see.

Hours later he was still there, his slumber a barrier that prevented him from hearing the trickling sound. It was the sound of water rising in the ditch.

This was a deep ditch. It went down a good twelve feet, its sides almost vertical where the crew of diggers had shoveled to reach a broken water pipe. They'd pulled it out a few days ago and shifted the flow to another pipe that ran parallel to the ditch a few feet away. They'd miscalculated the effect of the added pressure and the result was a leak in the second pipe. It was a small leak at first, but gradually it became wider and the water gained force going through the gap, presently coming through with the jet action of a garden hose turned on at full force. It loosened the soil and worked its way across four feet of mud and trickled merrily into the ditch.

When Bevan had fallen, he'd landed on his feet, then on his rump, rolling over gently in the soft mud. In his sleep he'd shifted from the face-down position and now he rested on his side. He was having a fine sleep down there in the mud in the twelve-foot

ditch. There was no dreaming, no fitful squirming or
quivering. He was motionless and completely asleep
and he didn't feel it when the water lapped against
his chin.

What woke him up was water getting into his nose.

He opened his eyes and lifted his head. In the
instant of feeling the wetness he thought he was in a
bathtub. But it can't be that, he thought. This isn't a
bathroom. And then, his senses rising quickly to full
wakefulness, It's a goddamn ditch and it's filling up
with water. Let's get the hell out of here.

He stood up. He was standing in two feet of water.
Now the water was coming in fast. He reached up for
a handhold to pull himself out and there was no
handhold.

Well now, he thought. Let's have a look at this.

He looked up, seeing the top of the ditch, which was
more than six feet above his head and seemed much
higher than that. Above it was the blackness of half past
eleven. Some of the glow from a three-quarter moon
was reflected on the shiny mud along the steep sides
where he was groping for a handhold. His hands
slipped away from the mud and he tried again. He kept
on trying and his hands kept slipping away.

Now the water was up past his knees.

He was walking along, telling himself the ditch had
to end somewhere and it wasn't anything to worry
about. He went twenty feet along the ditch, then thirty
feet, his hands feeling along the slick mud wall. He
walked another fifteen feet, going very slowly, telling
himself there was no need to hurry and soon he'd be at

the end of the ditch and climbing out. He tried to concentrate on that thought, pulling away from the other thought that told him the water was at his waist.

Minutes passed and he went walking along the ditch, staying close to the mud wall and groping for the handholds that weren't there. All at once he gave a jump that became another jump, a sort of convulsion as something furry hit his shoulder and refused to get off, its long tail flicking against his cheek. He took a swipe at it, and his hand struck a gray rodent face that opened its mouth and tried to get him with its fangs. He hit it again, and it gave a loud squeak and hopped off, making a big splash because it was a big one. He told himself it was a very big one and he tried to see it as it went swimming away. But now there was no moonlight, there was no light at all. There ought to be, he thought. The moon's up there and we ought to have some moonlight. He looked up and there was no moon, there were no stars. The blackness above his head was not the blackness of the sky. As he felt the water lapping at his chest he smelled the dank odor of weather-beaten wood. The odor came down from the planks they'd arranged across the top of the ditch in this section, where they'd used a pulley to lift the heavy pipe. That's what they did, he thought. They put planks up there, they built a bridge for themselves. But for this traveler down here it's no bridge, it's a ceiling. Or let's put it in the proper category and call it what it really is. You know damn well it's a trap.

The water was up to his chin. He was staring up at the ceiling of heavy planks that showed only the solid blackness, telling him there was no way out. Because now there was too much water and not enough time to get away from under the planks. He could move only by inches and there certainly wasn't enough time because the total darkness covered a wide area, telling him it was a very wide ceiling up there. It was wide enough to keep him trapped while the water kept rising so that eventually he'd float up, treading water and telling himself it was no use treading water, he wouldn't be going anywhere except up to the ceiling, where there'd soon be no air, only water.

Well? he asked himself. So what?

So isn't this what you wanted? Sure, it's a sloppy way to go out, but let's not get fussy and start finding fault with the method. The thing of it is, you're getting what you've been headed for, what you've been asking for, so there's no cause for complaint. But what the hell are you doing now? Why are you treading water?

It's a contradiction, that's what it is: You shouldn't be treading water. You should be standing here in the mud and letting the water go up past your eyes and the top of your head, with your mouth opened wide to take it into your lungs, doing it that way, the quick way. To get it over with so there'll be no more agony, no more anguish, no more singing the deep-down blues they've never composed because they can't find the lyrics to tell what it's like when you're a man but you're really not a man because you've lost it somewhere along the way and there's nothing you can do for her. Except let her go. Well, you did that, at least. You let her go. Very noble of you, really admirable. It's so

admirable it deserves a plaque. Maybe they'd hang it
on the wall at the Yale Club, telling new members to
read it and remember that fine gentleman who
stepped aside for the better man.

Then why are you trying to stay afloat?

It wasn't easy to tread water. His shoes felt awfully
heavy and the weight of his clothes was a drag on his
arms. Once he started to go down, he even tried to
stay down, but in the next moment he made a feverish
effort that lifted his head above the surface, his mouth
opened wide, greedy for air.

How come? he asked himself. What are you trying
to do?

Well, sure, you're trying to stay alive. But what for?
Say, that's an interesting question. It takes you back to
the Inspector, who failed to inspect deeply enough.
But let's not criticize the Inspector. After all, he had
nothing to work with. You remember the way he said
it, he said he hadn't bothered to make notes because
you didn't give him anything he could use. You went in
there and gave him something out of Hans Christian
Andersen, your slap-happy, rum-happy brain expecting
him to believe it, your spineless point of view hoping
fervently for the gallows to lift you and drop you and
get it over with in a jiffy.

Hey now. What is this? A showdown?

I guess so. I guess this is the time for it. They claim
there's always a time for it, the moment when a lamp
lights up inside and you can see it the way it is. Not
the way you thought it was, or what you thought you
thought it was, certainly not the booby-hatch thinking

that had you believing you merited the noose. This picture you see now is the true picture. It's right side up and it shows you what actually happened in the alley outside Winnie's Place, the man coming at you with the blackjack, and then when you used the broken bottle it was solely for the purpose of protecting yourself. So here and now we get rid of the billboard that tells of the destroyer who went out to spill some blood. Here and now we cancel that, and we replace it with what we hope will be some logic and common sense and normal thinking.

Oh, Christ, he thought. It's too late.

Because now there was the sound and the shock of his head bumping up against the underside of the wooden planks, the muddy water now rising to the twelve-foot limit so that there was no more air. There was only the water and the feeling of sinking, with the lungs aching for air, the brain throbbing with the water-clogged pattern that was somehow disconnected from himself because he wasn't thinking of himself as he began to battle the water, his body now horizontal and swimming several feet below the surface, going against the current that tried to keep him trapped under the wooden planks. He was thinking of someone he'd never seen, someone he'd never talked to, a man with whom he'd never communicated in any way, but who now cried out to him, Only you can save me.

He was thinking of Winnie's brother, Eustace.

I'm trying, he said to the Jamaican. I'm really trying now. And just then he came up, hoping there'd be no wooden planks, but his head hit the planks and he

went down again, his lungs lanced with flame that
climbed to blaze in his throat. He had his mouth
clamped so tightly that his teeth cut into the inner
walls, the blood lapping over and under his tongue.
What he wanted to do was to open his mouth, to let
the water in, so there'd be no more of the agony that
was just too much for a living creature to take. But he
heard Winnie's brother saying, Don't—don't— So he
kept his mouth closed, choking on the fire he couldn't
take but had to take while he gathered everything he
had for another try.

His arms hacked at the water and he kicked at it
and had the feeling he wasn't getting anywhere. Then
there was no feeling at all and he told himself he was
going down. But his arms and legs kept moving, taking him straight forward and then up. He heard the
Jamaican saying, Come on, come on. And it was as
though the dark-skinned hands were reaching for his
white-skinned wrists, taking hold and pulling him up
and away from the chamber of nothingness.

His head came up above the surface of the water
less than two feet away from the wooden planks. As
the air rushed into his gasping mouth, he hit the mud
wall, grabbed at the top of it and held on and climbed
over the side of the water-filled ditch. He rolled over a
few times, still trying to get away from the water that
wasn't there, still seeking the air he'd already found.
And then, resting on his back with his arms and legs
spread wide, he drifted out of it.

Chapter Thirteen

It was past three in the morning when Winnie heard knuckles rapping on the alley door. Without sound she said, Go away, mon. Dis place not open for business tonight. She pressed her face deeper into the pillow, wishing she could get some sleep. For hours she'd been trying to fall asleep, but there were too many thoughts and all of them were worries. With her eyes shut tightly she'd tried to pull away from it, but somehow it had the feel of a rope tied firmly around her chest, the other end of it out there in the darkness where it waited for her brother's neck.

The knocking came again, and then again. Winnie lifted her head from the pillow, emitting a groan mixed with an oath. She climbed out of the narrow bed that needed new springs and certainly needed a better mattress. She rubbed her hand against the small of her back, arching her spine to lessen the stiffness. The tattered nightgown flapped around her bare legs as she shuffled out of the room, going toward the alley door.

She reached for the doorknob, then decided against it. Whoever it was out there, he didn't deserve to be let in. He was very rude to come knocking on the door at this hour, when all the lights were out, and he ought to realize she wasn't selling drinks tonight. She turned away from the door and started back toward the tiny

room that was a combination bedroom-parlor-kitchen.
But then he hit the door again and called her name
and she recognized the voice.

Dat tourist, she thought. Dat clean-face American
from de high-class hotel. Coming here for more rum.
Coming here to seek de amusement, to look at comical
native woman and listen to comical way she talk. I give
him amusement, all right. Maybe I amuse him wid
broomstick alongside de head.

But instead of reaching for a broomstick, she opened
the door and started to say something unpleasant and
couldn't say anything because the sight of him was
unreal. He looked like something hauled out of a
swamp.

From head to toe he was covered with wet mud. He
stood there smiling dimly and it was like a cadaver
smiling. Winnie stepped back with her hand covering
her mouth. He murmured, "May I come in?" and she
nodded dazedly. He entered, saying, "Thank you," but
his politeness made it all the more unreal and Winnie
was trembling as she closed the door behind him.

She hurriedly switched on the light, and in the
glow from the ceiling bulbs she saw it was not an
apparition, just a mud-drenched man whose messy
appearance somehow blended with the battered
condition of the room. It was a kind of harmony, the
bedraggled man and the shambles of the room with
its littered floor and broken chairs and tables, the
splintered bar and smashed-in walls. Winnie told herself it was an altogether satisfactory picture. He not
clean-face now, she thought. Not wearing fine clothes

now. And de lesson of it is, when dey leave de fine hotel and come down to play in de mud, dey get muddy.

Then she wanted him to know what she was thinking. She folded her arms and leaned her head back and laughed at him.

He went on smiling dimly. He didn't say anything.

She laughed more loudly. "What happened, mon? How you get all dirtied up like dat?"

"I fell in a ditch."

Now she was laughing very loudly and holding her sides.

"It got filled up with water," he said.

"What a pity." She held her sides tightly and choked on the laughter. "I should have been dere to see it."

"Yes," he said. "It was really something. It was strictly Buster Keaton."

"Buster Keaton?"

"A famous clown." He wasn't smiling now. "Very famous in the silent-picture days."

"Tell me about him."

"Later," he said. "Right now I want—"

"I know what you want," she broke in. She'd stopped laughing, and the look on her face was stonily resentful. "You want more rum."

He shook his head very slowly.

"Of course you want more rum," Winnie said. "You want rum and amusement and much fun."

"Not now." He spoke quietly. "All I want now is information."

Winnie blinked a few times.

"I'm looking for someone," he said. "I'm looking for a man named Nathan Joyner."

She blinked again.

"Nathan Joyner," he repeated. "You know him? You know where I can find him?"

She didn't reply. Now her eyes were wary and defensive and she took a backward step.

"Please tell me," he said. "It's important. It concerns your brother."

She became rigid. Her hand came up slowly and her fingers pressed hard against the side of her face.

His tone was matter-of-fact as he started to tell her. He described what had happened in the alley the night before, and how it had become distorted in his mind, his thoughts veering away from logic and common sense and normal thinking, so that he'd visualized himself as a demon slayer rather than as a victim who had hit back. His voice quivered slightly as he went through that part of it, but then the quivering stopped and again he spoke matter-of-factly as he related the incident in the dining room of the Laurel Rock, where fifteen hundred dollars had changed hands. His tone remained level through all that and all the rest of it, all the way to the payoff at police headquarters, where the Inspector had said no sale. Then the only sound was Winnie's footsteps as she moved slowly across the room. She made her way past the broken chairs and tables, seated herself on the toolbox, and absently reached for the screwdriver on the floor. She played it from one hand to the other, then looked at it and saw what it was, the tool she'd tossed away earlier when she'd given up trying to make repairs. Her fingers tightened on the handle as she said, "Now dere is some hope. At least dere is a chance."

"Yes," he said. "But it's a thin one. And there's a time element."

"Time?" She looked at him. "How you mean?"

"Joyner," he said. "I've got to find him before he skips."

She frowned, not understanding.

And he said, "The man has fifteen hundred dollars. It isn't legitimate money. It's the kind of money that makes them jittery and they're always anxious to get out of town."

She shook her head slowly. She still didn't understand.

"I'm hoping he hasn't done it already," Bevan said, talking more to himself than to Winnie. "If he's still in town, and if I can find him—"

"But why you need Joyner? Why you not go to de Inspector and make de explanation?"

"The Inspector wouldn't believe it. He has me listed as Section Eight."

"Dat means what?"

"Goofy." He tapped the side of his head. "Sick up here."

"But if you tell de truth—"

"It wouldn't be enough, coming from me."

"Den I go wid you. I tell he—"

"That's out, Winnie. He'd show us the door. He'd think it was some silly stunt you'd cooked up to save your brother."

"If you would insist—"

"But he wouldn't listen. There's only one way I can get him to listen. I've got to show him the proof. That's where Joyner comes in."

"Wid a statement?"

"With more than a statement. Joyner has his hands on the concrete evidence. He has the blackjack and the bottle."

So then she caught the drift of it. She nodded slowly. But now her frown was deepened and her eyes were dulled with doubt and worry. She said, "It discouraging, dis situation. It very discouraging. I sorry to say it, but I tink you face impossible task. It hopeless to expect dat Joyner will—" and she couldn't find the word.

"Cooperate?"

"Yes. Cooperate." She shook her head dismally. "You go to Joyner wid de request and he will laugh at you."

"But if I can—"

"Dere nothing you can do wid Joyner. I know dat mon. I know what he is. He is trickster, a rascal who hide de tricks under friendly smile and quiet polite talk. You know dere is no way you can appeal to he heart."

"Yes, I know that," Bevan said. "I know it needs something more practical."

"Money?"

"No," he said. "Money wouldn't do it. He's got a bankroll now. He can afford to be independent."

"Den how you manage it?"

He was smiling thinly, giving her the answer with his eyes.

It caused her to wince slightly. She said, "Mon, I not recommend dat method."

"Neither do I," he murmured. "But the fact is, it appears to be the only way."

"It might lead you to grief, mon. You attempt to use force, you take serious risk."

He shrugged again. He didn't say anything.

Winnie said, "I tell you, mon, it perilous thing. Dis Joyner, he slick one, and if it come to violence, he not easily subdued. I have seen what he can do wid knife."

"He carries a knife?"

"Always."

"And he's an expert?"

"Like a snake wid fangs."

"That's interesting."

"And you?" she asked. "Can you use knife?"

"Only to cut bread. Or cheese."

"Please, mon. It not funny."

"You're telling me?"

"Perhaps if you had pistol—"

"No," he said. "I might be forced to use it. I wouldn't want that to happen. I'm not looking to hurt him. I just want to bring him around to my point of view."

"How you do dat? It need more dan talk."

He nodded slowly. Then he looked at his hands. He

clenched his right hand and hit it lightly against the palm of his left.

"Dat way?" Winnie asked.

"It's worth a try," he said.

"But how you expect to—"

"Maybe I'll have luck," he said. And then, aloud to himself, "If I can get in close, get him before he's ready for it, just to put him in the right mood, sort of dizzy but not too dizzy, I mean just dizzy enough to see things my way…"

Winnie shook her head again. She sighed heavily.

He grinned, as if he wanted to cheer her up a little. He said, "That's all it needs, Winnie. Just a little luck."

Winnie said, "You cannot do it alone. You need some men to help you."

"What men?"

"I could wake up several of my neighbors. Dey would be glad to—"

"But that would ruin it," he said. "Too many cooks, et cetera. If Joyner saw me coming in with other men, he'd know right away it was strong-arm stuff. If he's fast and tricky, as you say he is, he'd know how to handle that. So what it needs here is some cute maneuvering. I've got to catch him off guard, and then move in and try to tag him."

"Wid what? Wid dose?" And she gestured almost angrily at his two hands, which were now unclenched and dangled from mud-covered arms attached to wearily slumping shoulders. She was looking him up and down, and she was seeing a sad excuse for a would-be combatant. "What chance you got?"

"A chance to try."

There was something in his tone that caused her to focus on his eyes. Then very slowly she lifted herself from the toolbox. She stood very close to him and spoke in a whisper. "Why you do dis? Why take dis terrible risk?"

"It—" But whatever it was, he couldn't put it into words.

"Dere is possibility you will lose your life. You realize dat?"

He nodded slowly.

"Den why you make dis attempt dat might put you in de grave? Why you not go back to hotel, where you—"

"Where I belong?"

"Yes," she said. Then something caused her to talk faster and louder, the words shooting out like pellets. "Dat is your place, mon. Dat is your category. I make de sensible suggestion you go back dere."

"What's Joyner's address?"

"In morning you wake up and it is all forgotten. You sit down and have delicious breakfast in de elegant dining room."

"Tell me where I can find him."

"You put on de fine clothes and show de clean face to all de other clean-face tourist."

"Tell me." He grabbed her arm.

She shook her head. She locked her lips tightly.

"Goddamn it," he muttered, and his hand tightened on her arm. "Come on, spill it," he said, but she let out a groan, she would not speak. So then he let go of her and turned away slowly, moving toward the alley door. At the door he turned again and said, "Please—give me a break."

It was as though his eyes were reaching into her and pulling it from her lips, the house number and the name of the street. Her voice was toneless as she told him how to find the street.

"Thank you," he said. "Thank you very much."

He walked out. Winnie stood there looking at the alley door. For some moments her face was expressionless. But then she felt something in her hand, and she gazed downward and saw it there, the screwdriver gripped firmly at her side. Dis tool, she thought, dis tool dat is made to repair what needs to be repaired. Then she was lifting the screwdriver and holding it high, like a torch. The ceiling light glinted on the metal shaft, and the glow bounced off and poured into her eyes. In that instant her eyes were lit, her face was radiant, and she knew why she'd given him the address of the man he wanted to find. Without sound she said, He is one of us. His skin is white, but dat is no matter. He is trying to make repairs and he is one of us.

Chapter Fourteen

Seven and three and seventeen. Keep the numbers in mind, he thought. But you're getting dizzy again and you might forget. No you won't do that. You can't allow yourself to forget. It's seven and three and seventeen. It's seven blocks east on Barry Street and turn right into what she said was Morgan's Alley. Then stay on the left-hand side and pass three intersections and the house number is seventeen. And will you please get a move on?

He tried to walk faster but the wet clothes held him back. The dampness had penetrated his flesh and seeped into his bones, mixing with the fatigue that now told him it was a matter of stamina and he didn't have that kind of stamina. The water-filled ditch had played him out. But then you slept, he thought. Well, yes, but you didn't sleep long enough, and when you woke up you went for a walk that was more of a hike, trying to find Barry Street and Winnie's Place.

Come on, keep walking. That's right. That's fine. You'll make it. Anyway, I think you'll make it. You didn't think you'd make it to Winnie's Place but you got there, didn't you? So you did it then and you can do it now. If only you'll keep walking. That's it. Sure, it's easy. It's a cinch. Oh, Christ, I'm so tired. So wet and tired and getting dizzy and dizzier....

Oh, no, you won't. You won't sit down on that doorstep. It looks awfully tempting and it's for free, but if you accept the invitation you'll find it's extremely expensive. It'll be your head falling on your chest, your eyes closing while you fade away from everything. During which interval our friend Nathan fades away from Kingston with his fifteen hundred dirty dollars. And our chance to bat for Eustace fades away like a hand waving goodbye. So you won't sit down on that doorstep. You'll keep walking.

Keep walking and remember it's seven and three and seventeen. Or is it nineteen? No, it's seventeen. You see? You can still think straight. But I wish you could walk straight. Just look at the way you're walking. Your legs are moving like Sugar Ray's on that summer night when he met Maxim, but it wasn't Maxim getting him, it was July getting him in the twelfth round and he barely made it to his corner. It was a pity he couldn't come out for the thirteenth. But what about you? You'll be lucky if you can answer the bell for round one.

It almost gets a laugh. I mean, you're banged up before it even starts. It's really silly to expect that you can do anything, the shape you're in. A nine-year-old could tag you with a left and you'd go down. Like a wet sack.

Really wet through. All that muddy water you took a bath in. And some of it you must have swallowed. Well, it was time you drank some water. But I can think of pleasanter ways to go on the wagon. All right, we'll take up that matter at the next meeting. That is, if there'll be a next meeting. The way things are going, we might be adjourning for the season. Or maybe for all future seasons, considering what she said about Nathan's talent with a knife.

I'm getting there, Eustace. Now we've made five and it's two more blocks to go and then turn right and Did I hear something?

You sure did, mister.

He wanted to stop walking. He told himself it would be a mistake to stop walking, a serious mistake to turn and look around. The footsteps coming on made the kind of noise that told him they were trying not to make noise. There were two of them, maybe three of them. They must have been waiting in some doorway, waiting there for any damn fool to come walking along at this hour when all the lights were out, probably hoping it would be a drunken seaman with money in his pockets and no caution at all in his brain. Better yet, this target they had was a staggering mess that appeared half dead in the wet, muddy clothes.

For a split moment he thought yearningly of years and years ago at Yale, when they gave him the blue sweater with the white Y because he could run the half mile in one minute fifty-four seconds flat. But you can't run now, he thought. You can't even try to run. You have no legs.

Then what can you do?

There isn't a goddamn thing you can do and you know it. Now you have it checked, it's three of them, and you can bet they're properly equipped. It's bullets or blades or something heavy that'll bash your skull and now they're coming in closer.

But don't get peeved about it. Don't get irritated. Maybe we can play some pinochle, make some sort of bid that'll hold them off for a moment. So then he thought of the Bank of Nova Scotia, where he'd cashed the travelers' checks, and his hand went to the pocket where he kept his wallet. He did that very fast, pivoting hard in the same instant to face the three Jamaicans, who came in crouching low, two of them with bread knives and the third with an ice pick. They were young and wore rags and looked very hungry and malicious. But the sight of the wallet had them stalled and they straightened and stood motionless while he opened the wallet to show them the thick sheaf of bills inside. Then he tossed the wallet at their feet.

The one with the ice pick was stopped and reaching for the wallet. The others made a double-flank maneuver that put Bevan in the middle. He told himself not to look at the knives or the ice pick. He was focusing on the wallet, seeing the bills coming out, the Jamaican making a quick count.

"How much?" one of them said.

"Considerable," the counter said. "About sixty guineas."

"Dat not bad."

But the counter wasn't satisfied. He pointed toward Bevan's left arm, then pointed down toward the wrist that showed the gray suede strap and the white-gold case. Bevan took off the wrist watch and handed it to him. Immediately he lifted it to his ear and held it there and then he frowned and said, "It not go."

"It got wet," Bevan said.

"What else you have?"

"Nothing."

"Display de honds."

He lifted his hands to display his fingers. There were no rings on his fingers.

"Now de pockets."

He reversed his pockets, taking out a wet handkerchief and a water-ruined pack of cigarettes and a book of matches.

"Now loosen de pants."

"What for?"

"So I can look. I see if you wear money belt."

He lowered his pants and then his underpants and the three of them moved in close to see if he was carrying additional cash around his middle. They stayed in very close while he showed them there was nothing. And then, while he zipped up his trousers, they moved in even closer and he knew they meant to put him away. He thought, They want to be sure I won't go to the police and give their descriptions. That's part of it, and the other part is the malice. The general idea is they don't care much for tourists. And that winds it up, I suppose. That makes it fundamental. They're warriors and they're dealing with the foe. It's justice, in a way. It sort of balances the equation. They've been kicked around so much, and whenever they have a chance to kick back, they make the most of it. Can't blame them for that.

He didn't know it, but he was smiling at them. It was a soft and somewhat sad smile, his head slanted just a little in a plaintive sort of way, his eyes saying, I don't feel sorry for myself. It's just a damn shame for Winnie's brother.

The ice pick was aimed at Bevan's belly. But the hand that held the ice pick now trembled slightly, and the Jamaican took a backward step, frowning uncertainly at the others, who were also stepping back and lowering their bread knives. Then the three of them opened their mouths to say something and couldn't say anything. Bevan stood motionless, the moonlight glowing on his face, bathing the smile he didn't know was there. The one with the ice pick was saying, "Why you look at us like dat?"

He didn't answer. He didn't know what the man meant.

"As if you not afraid," the Jamaican said. "As if us your friends."

He nodded slowly.

"But if us kill you—"

"You're still my friends."

"Me not understand," the Jamaican said. He had loosened his grip on the ice pick.

"Me understand," one of the others said. "Me know what de mon try now. He try be clever."

"Me disagree," the one with the ice pick said. "Me tink he mean what he say. Me tink de mon say it from here," and he hit his hand against his chest.

"Den what us do wid him?"

"Us let him go."

"And give him chance to—"

"Us let him go." The one with the ice pick spoke very quietly. "Me cannot slay a mon who looks at me like dat."

Then he beckoned to the others as he turned away. They hesitated for a moment and he beckoned again, saying, "Come on, come on," as though he wanted to get away from there in a hurry, before he changed his mind. They were following him, the three of them now walking away from Bevan, who was shaking his head slowly because he couldn't believe what he was seeing.

But there they go, he said to himself. And it isn't as though you bluffed them or foxed them. You weren't trying to be cute. Then what was it? What the hell was it? Well, whatever it was, it worked. So now let's get moving again. It's two blocks to Morgan's Alley and then turn right and— I sure wish you knew what it was that got you out of that jam. He said it was the way you were looking at him. What did he mean? What did he read in your face? I think this is getting a little too mystical and we'd better bring it back to the practical terms of knowing it's finished business. Let's drop it and get on with our social plans for the evening. But what's this? What's happening to your legs? You're walking straighter now. You're walking faster.

It wasn't really rapid walking. But it was much faster than before. He moved steadily in a straight path along the moonlit paving of Barry Street, coming to the final intersection and turning right to enter Morgan's Alley.

Chapter Fifteen

It was an alley of hovels, mostly of splintered, rotted wood, some of them roofed with tar paper, and some put together with rusty sheet metal picked up on the docks. The people who lived in these dwellings paid no rent or real-estate taxes. The rental value was zero and it was useless to tax them; there was no way to assess this property.

It was just a strip of dried mud and accumulated ashes and all sorts of rubbish, including the bones of cats devoured by mongrels. Or sometimes the cats were eaten by swarms of rats which came to this area looking for garbage and couldn't find any because in the area there was an acute shortage of food and therefore all plates were scraped shining clean. Yet some of these citizens made money.

They made it selling certain wares that couldn't be displayed in an open marketplace. The old ones sold their powers of Obeah to whoever believed in this type of witchcraft and wished to hurt an enemy or erase him entirely. There were some who sold opium they'd obtained at bargain prices from seamen who'd sneaked it out of Asia. If it wasn't opium it was hemp, and they had a way of treating it to make it extra-powerful, lifting the smoker very high above the earth, allowing him to soar up there with all the great ones, all the famous singers and dancers, all the champions

and leaders. This special hemp they sold along
Morgan's Alley was a very pleasant habit when it was
available. When it was not available, the loss of altitude was sudden, a sort of plunging, and so finally they
had to take it all the way and jump off a pier. Or sometimes they ignited themselves with matches. Another
popular method was wrapping a cloth very tightly
around the head to cover the nose and mouth so one
couldn't breathe. It was the only thing to do when the
hemp was not available to a user.

But various other problems were easier to handle.
For those who needed some special type of female,
Morgan's Alley met most of these requirements. It was
not a matter of looks. The women were mostly sorry-
looking specimens who'd been turned down by the
pimps and madams of Barry Street. So they learned
some unusual techniques that put them in the off-
beam category. They learned these capers when they
were young, and when they were older they were
artists at it and had their steady customers, some of
whom traveled thousands of miles for just one night in
Morgan's Alley. For instance, a certain Canadian lum-
berman worth millions, known throughout the Empire
as a distinguished gentleman and sportsman. At forty-
six he was built like a Rugby player, and he could have
modeled for athletic supporters. And he had a fine-
looking wife and four fine-looking girls, two of them
married and with children. They all adored him. Twice
each year he made the flight to Jamaica and registered
at an exclusive hotel near Montego Bay. He put in a
few days playing golf, doing some fishing, and then

quietly hired a car and went off alone, his luggage consisting of a tattered bag filled with very old clothes. Arriving in Kingston, he'd wait until after midnight, then get dressed in the old clothes and come here to Morgan's Alley, to the house where she had his letter and was waiting for him. She was past sixty and stood four-feet-nine and weighed eighty-three pounds. The first thing he'd do was give her the money. In American currency it was some fifty dollars. Then she told him to give her a manicure, and he obeyed. He polished her fingernails to exquisite brightness, then did the same to her toenails. She rewarded him with a kick in the face. Not a hard kick, really; not enough to cause a broken nose or mashed lips; just hard enough to cause his head to throb, to give him the dull pain he'd been deliciously anticipating for six months up there in Canada. And that was all. Without saying good night he'd open the door and walk out, and next day he'd be in the plane flying north. Of course, she didn't know who he was, but that didn't matter in the least. What mattered was the fifty dollars that she could live on for months. It never occurred to her that he'd be willing to pay many times that amount. She didn't know he'd searched four continents to find the face and body that resembled the image in his mind. He'd found her nine years ago, and since then these twice-a-year trips to Morgan's Alley were the most important functions of his life.

In another hovel there was a young woman whose most dependable customer was an Australian named Hainesworth. He was first mate on a merchant vessel that sailed into Kingston Harbour at least five times a year. He was in his early forties and was slightly over six feet tall and weighed close to three hundred pounds. The young woman weighed around 110. He paid her the equivalent of ten dollars to walk out of the shack and then come back in and find him there, and then pretend to be terribly frightened while he grinned hungrily and moved toward her. Then she had to pretend to fight him off while he ripped at her clothes, threw her to the floor, the agreement being that she could fight any way she wanted to, with scratching or biting or whatever damage she cared to inflict. He was not permitted to hit back; not with his fists, anyway. The rules stipulated that he could grapple with her, try to subdue her with his weight, and naturally he always managed to do just that, so that when it finally happened it was as close to actual rape as it could possibly be. She was a good little actress and to a certain extent it wasn't acting. She enjoyed trying to hold him off and hurting him while she did it. One night some years ago she'd scarred him for life, biting a rather large chunk of flesh from his chin. He'd bled something awful. But he hadn't been angry with her. After all, it was part of the agreement.

Tonight he was very angry with her. She hadn't been there when he'd arrived. Now he waited there in the alley, scowling at the locked door, cursing her for being late, then worrying that maybe she wouldn't show at all, and then cursing her again because she knew how much he needed this, he couldn't do without it. He thought of all the long weeks at sea when he'd squirmed in his bunk, impatient for the day when the ship would reach Kingston, which meant Morgan's Alley and the only solace for his three hundred pounds of flabby flesh and bulbous face, which females couldn't bear to look at.

Hainesworth lifted a sweating palm to his sweating face, rubbing trembling fingers across his trembling mouth. He took out a large pocket watch from his white duck trousers and looked at the dial, which showed five minutes past four. Then he looked up at the black sky, which would start to get light in a couple of hours. He sighed heavily, leaning against the doorway of the hovel, and then his mouth tightened and he cursed her again. But the oaths were no help. The oaths only increased the sweating and the trembling. She won't show, he thought, She's gone off somewhere and she won't show. A bloody, rotten way to treat me that's been so fair and decent with her. All the pound notes she's been getting. And that necklace I sent her from Melbourne. Another time from Melbourne it was a bracelet. And then from Tortola I do it up real fancy and air-mail a box of sweets along with the note that tells her I'll arrive within a week. Well, you bloody well spoiled her, you did. Necklace and bracelet and box of sweets. You ought to break down the door.

He stepped away from the splintered door of the hovel, aiming his bulk at it, bracing himself for the lunge that would send him crashing through the flimsy barrier. But then he changed his mind. The only thing he wanted in there was the female, and she wasn't

there. What you might as well do, he thought, is walk
on down the alley to Hannah's where you can sit down
and have some ale and pay her an extra few shillings
for another look at them pictures. But he'd already
been in and out of Hannah's several times tonight, and
besides, he was tired of looking at Hannah's collection
of pictures, the pencil sketches made by her nephew
who'd been to an art school but couldn't sell his land-
scapes and therefore veered off to the type of art that
is never displayed in licensed galleries. Hannah's
nephew had sold quite a few of these pictures before
the authorities caught up with him, the judge giving
him eighteen months. But Hannah had managed to
salvage some of his work and she insisted these were
the best of the lot, the price is only a shilling for a
fifteen-minute rental, a special price of three shillings
for an hour. And please do not offer to buy dese
pictures, dey are not for sale. One time a mon he tries
to steal dem and now I have two of his finger in a jar of
vinegar. Look, I show you. I keep de jar as a reminder
to each and all dat dese pictures are my property, and
even though I am an old woman sick wid de rheuma-
tism, I am capable of dealing wid any rascal who
attempts to—

Hainesworth chuckled softly, thinking of Hannah,
whose age was seventy-three, whose weight was ap-
proximately the same because she took very little
nourishment and it was said she seldom slept. For
some moments he managed to amuse himself with
the thought of Hannah, but then the thought took

him again to the pictures, to one in particular, which
showed a gorilla and a girl. It was an accurately scaled
drawing and it was done in detail. The gorilla was
immense and the girl was small and delicately formed,
her slim legs kicking frenziedly as she writhed in the
grasp of the hairy arms. Then in Hainesworth's mind
the picture moved and he saw it happening, except
that now the gorilla wore a first mate's cap and on his
left arm there was an anchor tattooed. He heard a
hissing sound that was his own breath indrawn between his teeth and somewhat spasmodically he put
his hands in his trouser pockets. He wasn't feeling for
what was in the pockets and his hands went in deeper,
his bulbous face twitching as he told himself to stop it.
He managed to stop it, although the effort caused him
to bite his lip, and when his hands came out of his
pockets he was sagging against the doorway of the
hovel. The decayed wood groaned under the pressure
of his weight. The sound made a sort of counterpoint
with the groan coming from very deep inside him. He
thought, You're in a bad way, chappie. It's really bad
and it's getting worse by the minute. Well, this just
won't do, this waiting here. I think you'd better go
back to the Seamen's House and climb into bed until
you feel better.

But that won't do, either. You know you wouldn't be
able to sleep. You'd bite the pillow to shreds, the way
you did that time in Melbourne when you followed the
woman for I don't know how many city blocks, and
finally she saw you and started to run, and you went

back to your room and ruined the pillow, the stuffing spilling out over the place, the next day the landlady raised an awful row. So let's not go back to the Seamen's House. Let's wait here a while. Just a little while longer. She'll show. She's bound to come along sooner or later. And when she does...

He rubbed his sweating palms together and licked his lips, smiling wetly and then very widely as he heard the footsteps approaching.

But it wasn't the woman. In Hainesworth's eyes it was a living zero covered with mud. The Australian gave a grunt of disappointment and disgust. He scowled at the straggler who was using the moonlight that poured along this side of the alley and put a blue-silver glow on the doorways. The man was squinting at the doors as though searching for an address. On some of the doors the numbers were marked with chalk, but there was no number on this door, and there were several neighboring dwellings also unnumbered.

"Which one you want?" Hainesworth asked.

"Seventeen."

"It's down that way."

"I know it is. I've been counting the houses. But I lost count."

"This one's twenty-nine," Hainesworth said.

"Thanks," Bevan said, and he started to move on at once.

The Australian walked toward him. "Who you looking for?"

"A friend," Bevan said. He kept moving.

Hainesworth came up and walked along beside him and said, "What's the hurry, chappy?"

Bevan didn't answer. He wasn't looking at the big flabby Australian. He was counting the doorways.

And then Hainesworth was standing in front of him, blocking his path and saying loudly, "Who lives in Seventeen?"

"Winston Churchill."

"You think that's funny, chappy?"

"No," Bevan said. He started to edge past the Australian, who moved with him and again blocked his path. He gave a little sigh and said, "I really can't talk to you now. I'm in a hurry."

"For what?" Hainesworth had his arms folded. He was looking the straggler up and down, seeing the straw-colored hair and the gray eyes and telling himself that underneath all that mud it was a white man wearing fairly expensive clothes. A tourist, he decided. An American tourist. It might be interesting to chat with him a while. At any rate, it's a way to pass the time while I'm waiting for my lady. But he doesn't seem inclined to chat. He's rather unsociable, I'd say. Shall we move aside and let him pass? He said he was in a hurry. But he's smaller than you are, he's considerably smaller. I think we'll have some fun with this one.

So then the Australian repeated the question but didn't get an answer. He smiled at the American and said, "Why can't you tell me? You afraid?"

"No," Bevan said. "Just tired. You're making me tired, mister."

"Really?" Hainesworth tightened the smile, then let it fade, with his chest expanding as he said, "You know, chappy, I don't think I care for that remark."

"Then I'll take it back. I apologize."

"That's better."

"Of course it is. But you know something? You're a terrible bore, and I wish you'd get out of the way."

"Tell me something, chappy. Suppose I don't?"

"If you don't," Bevan said slowly, "you're going to be very sorry."

Hainesworth laughed. It was harsh, derisive laughter, and he liked the sound of it, and he made it again, and louder.

Bevan shoved him.

It wasn't much of a shove. It only pushed him back a step or two. But the laughter was choked in his throat and somehow he couldn't breathe. He saw the smaller man moving toward him and he took another backward step and then another. He went on doing that as the smaller man walked toward him, coming very slowly. "Don't," he gasped. "Don't!" seeing something in the smaller man's eyes that told him his only move was to turn fast and make a run for it. As he pivoted, he lost his balance and fell sideways, landing with a thud in the dried mud of the alley. He gasped again and no words came out. He was trying to roll away and he couldn't move. His eyes were shut tightly so he wouldn't see it coming, the kick in the face or something worse. Something much worse, he told himself, feeling his fat belly quivering against the hard-packed mud of the alley.

But nothing happened. He heard the footsteps going away and he rolled over and looked and saw the smaller man walking slowly through the darkness, the straw-colored hair glinting in the moonlight.

Hainesworth lifted himself to his feet and moved off quickly in the opposite direction. He was telling himself he'd got off easily, he was very lucky. But as he came up to the doorway of the woman's dwelling, he sagged and went to his knees and let out a grinding sob. You jellyfish, he said to himself. You yellow-bellied jellyfish. What were you scared of? It was just a man. And maybe that's the point of it. You were dealing with a man. A real man. And you? You're just a—

But let's drop it. Let's think of something pleasant. Like knowing there's another way to assert your maleness, a much easier way, and certainly much more enjoyable. Just tell yourself she'll soon be here, and then…His glazed eyes looked down at his large hands, the sweat glimmering in his cupped palms, the fat fingers bent and clawing hungrily.

Chapter Sixteen

We're too late, Bevan thought. He stood facing the dark windows and the locked door. There was no number on the door, but he knew for sure this was 17. He'd counted the other doorways very carefully and this had to be 17. But it might as well be zero, he told himself. There's nobody home.

He had knocked on the door and then he'd kicked it, and when there'd been no response he'd pressed his ear against the doorway, straining to hear the slightest sound from inside the hovel. There was no sound, and the stillness in the alley was like a message saying goodbye and signed "Nathan."

Yes, Bevan thought, he took the fifteen hundred dollars and skipped while the skipping was good. From here on in it's better meals for Mr. Joyner, better clothes and finer barbershops and certainly a considerably finer residence.

Well, we tried. We loused it up and then we tried to fix it. Is that a consoling thought? I don't think so. It certainly doesn't help Eustace. But then, there's no way to help Eustace. Nothing you can do now. It's too late, that's all. It's too late because what it needed was Joyner and now there's no Joyner and of course that's your fault. If you'd come here earlier, or if—

Let's not start with the ifs. It's bad enough without

bringing in the ifs. Please limit yourself to the facts, the facts being that you came here to see Nathan and you knocked on the door and the door wouldn't open. But what's this coming out?

It was smoke. It was a very thin ribbon of green-blue smoke seeping from the doorway. The moonlight made a cross current, the glow slanting across the path of the smoke that came out from the narrow gap between door and sill. It's really smoke, he told himself. Something's burning in there. Then he caught the aroma of it and at first he thought it was tobacco, but another whiff suggested it was more potent than tobacco. In the next instant he knew what it was. His mind went back to Fiftieth Street and Tenth Avenue, to a certain night in Hallihan's when a party of joy-poppers had lit up their sticks and the bartender had said very quietly, "Not in here you don't. You take that junk outside or I'll call the law and you'll do at least a year."

So it's weed, Bevan thought. He's in there smoking weed with the lights out, which means he's been on it for a good many hours, fading into the pleasant semi-sleep that prevented him from hearing the knocking on the door. And then he came out of it to light up again. Maybe now we can let him know he has a visitor.

He knocked on the door. He hit it very hard and then again, and he went on doing it until his knuckles hurt from the impact. For more than a minute nothing happened. Then he saw the glow from an orange-tinted bulb, a spreading stream of dim light playing on the windows. He heard the slow footsteps coming toward the door, saw the door opening, saw the weed-fogged eyes and the smiling mouth.

The smoke was curling up from the handmade job that Joyner held delicately between thumb and fore-finger, holding it close to his lips to get the fumes even when he wasn't inhaling. His face was enveloped in the green-blue cloud.

"Having a party?" Bevan murmured.

Joyner nodded. He went on smiling. It seemed he didn't recognize the visitor. For a brief moment his listless eyes met Bevan's eyes, and then he gazed past Bevan as though Bevan weren't there. He put the stick of hemp in his mouth and took a slow charge of smoke through his teeth, making a hissing sound as he sucked it in, his lips opened slightly, mixing it with just enough air to get the right blend. As it went in, as the blast hit him, he grimaced in the throes of unendurable delight.

"Is it that good?" Bevan said.

The Jamaican didn't reply. He turned slowly and went inside the one-room hovel, leaving the door open. Bevan followed him in and closed the door.

It was like a steam room. The fumes from countless sticks of hemp were rising to the ceiling and coming down and going up again. The smoke was so thick that he wondered seriously if there was enough oxygen to sustain life. He coughed a few times, then he hurried to the nearest window and opened it halfway.

He heard Joyner saying, "What are you doing?"

"We need some air in here."

"The air spoils it," Joyner said. "Please close the window."

Bevan was leaning out the window and coughing out the fumes and trying to pull some fresh air into his lungs.

"I wish you'd close the window," Joyner said quietly and politely. "You're letting all the birds out of the cage."

"Birds?"

"The pretty birds," Joyner said. "You can't see them, but they're here. They fly around so slowly, so graceful, and they're such pleasant companions. I like them because they never chirp loudly, or chatter and argue like the sparrows. They just fly around and sing in a soft chorus, a selection of lullabies."

Bevan closed the window. He told himself there was no use in debating the point. It was a minor issue and he wasn't here to debate minor issues. He thought, We'll just have to get used to the fumes, that's all.

He turned and looked at Joyner, who sat on the edge of a narrow cot, his face glinting in the dim glow from the orange-tinted bulb. The bulb was set in an unshaded lamp on a small table near the cot. On the floor at the side of the cot there was a scattering of stubs from the sticks of weed. The sticks had been thoroughly smoked and the stubs were tiny. Bevan counted them for some moments and then lost count. He heard Joyner saying something about the birds again and then it became a meaningless mumble that had to do with flowers borrowed from a garden on the planet Venus and from there it was an inaudible murmur.

Bevan was leaning against the wall near the window and glancing around the room. Instead of chairs there were a couple of fruit boxes. Instead of a carpet there were some old newspapers spread on the floor. On the other side of the room he saw a wooden contraption placed near a hole where the wall met the floor. He focused on it and saw it was a homemade rat trap. In the space between the rat trap and the edge of the cot there was a battered suitcase resting on its side and some of the contents had spilled out. There were a few shirts and socks and a pale-green short-sleeved sport shirt. That tells me something, he thought. That tells me he started to pack and then it occurred to him he could use a charge of hemp. He's really a user and the immediate need for hemp was more important than taking off.

So let's say he went out and bought a stick or two and came back here and started to blast. It was fine while it lasted but it didn't lift him high enough and he went out and bought some more. I guess he'd been without it for a long time, but then he got his hands on fifteen hundred dollars and he could buy all the hemp he wanted. Instead of merely taking off from Kingston, he took off from the planet and went up there to Venus with his friends the birds, who guide him toward that garden where he borrowed the flowers, which of course mean more weed. Look at him sitting there working on it. Look at him gaining altitude. Maybe it'll make him easy to handle. Or harder to handle, considering the fact that it's a stimulant and it leads them to believe they're tops at doing anything at all. Well, anyway, let's find out. Let's see what Nathan has to offer.

He moved toward the cot and said, "You know who I am?"

Joyner gave him the dreary smile and didn't say anything.

"I'm the customer," Bevan said. "I bought something from you this morning. It cost fifteen hundred dollars to buy it."

The Jamaican didn't say anything. The dreamy smile was going away. And then his face showed no expression at all. He sat there looking at Bevan as though there were an information desk between them and he was waiting for the clerk to provide additional facts.

Bevan took another step toward the cot. Now he was halfway across the room. He said to himself, Keep talking, and for Christ's sake get him interested in what you're saying. Get him off guard so that when you're close enough you can haul off and—

He said, "You recall the transaction? It was in the Laurel Rock, in the dining room. I was having a late breakfast and you came to my table."

"Yes, I remember," Joyner said softly. He looked down at the half-smoked stick of weed in his fingers. "This smoke is not what you think it is. It doesn't diminish the memory. On the contrary, it's like a strip of microfilm, and when the strip is long enough I can memorize a dictionary."

Bevan gestured toward the weed. "What else does it do?"

"It's like a supercharger," Joyner said. "The power potential is limitless. I recommend it to all athletes and soldiers and manual laborers."

He really believes that, Bevan thought.

The Jamaican said, "It also gives the brain a boost. It should be used in universities and chemical laboratories and certainly in legislative assemblies."

"They ought to put it on the market."

"Yes, they ought to," Joyner said. "But they won't. It would put the distilleries out of business. Another thing, there's no way to tax it or control the price. It grows everywhere."

"Like grass?"

"It comes up faster than grass," Joyner said. "If they made it a legal commodity, we'd all be growing it and using it and thriving on it. We'd all be living again in the Garden of Eden."

"That would be nice."

"It certainly would," Joyner said. "But of course it can never happen. We exist in a world of restrictions which could not allow it."

"You're so right," Bevan said. He took another step toward the cot.

"Don't do that," Joyner murmured.

"Do what?"

"Don't come any closer."

"Why not?" And he was smiling amiably and moving slowly toward the Jamaican and thinking, We're almost there, just a few more steps…

"Restrictions," Joyner said. Then his arm was just a blur, it happened that fast. His hand was empty for a split second and in the same instant there was a knife in his hand.

Bevan stood motionless. He heard a slight clicking noise and he saw a six-inch blade shooting out from the mother-of-pearl handle.

"What's that for?" he asked.

"Security."

"But I only came here to talk."

"Then talk."

"Not with that thing pointed at my gizzard."

"Does it worry you?"

"Sure it worries me. It scares the hell out of me. I wish you'd put it away."

"You mean make it vanish?"

Bevan didn't reply. He was looking at the glittering blade and thinking, I've never seen it done like that. I've seen it done in the movies and once at a circus sideshow and they did it very fast but not that fast.

Joyner took another drag at the hemp. He hauled it in very deep and held it and murmured, "Watch this." Then again his arm was a blur and the knife vanished.

"Where did it go?" Bevan asked.

"It didn't go far."

"But where is it?"

"Here," Joyner said. He did it faster than before. It was so fast that he didn't seem to be moving his arm, just sitting there showing the knife in his hand.

Bevan shook his head slowly. "Beats me."

"I started young," Joyner said. He repeated the action with the knife. It vanished and appeared and vanished again. Then the dreamy smile came back to his face and he sipped more smoke from the hemp.

So there it is, Bevan thought. There you have it. Well, you were warned about this. Winnie told you. Only thing is, it was an understatement. He pulls out that knife faster than you can blink. But don't get jittery. Please don't get jittery.

He heard the Jamaican saying, "Please sit down, Mr. Bevan. Make yourself comfortable."

He didn't move. He was standing just a few feet away from the cot. For a moment he played with the idea of lunging at Joyner, and his arm tingled with the urge to swing, his right hand throbbing because he wanted it to be a fist crashing against the man's jaw. His eyes were focused on the man's face, narrowing the focus to the jaw, and then the precise target area, close to the chin, where his knuckles could hit the important vein that connected with the brain. But of course it wouldn't happen that way. No matter how quickly he did it, the knife would be quicker.

Joyner made a friendly and hospitable gesture toward one of the fruit boxes. Bevan went to the box and sat down on it. He crossed his legs and wrapped his folded hands around his knees. Through the green-blue curtain of smoke he saw the orange glow slanting across the smiling face of Joyner. The colors and shadows had a Gauguin touch; it was really like a portrait by Gauguin. Or perhaps a still life, he thought. That face doesn't look human. The eyes are like camera lenses. An X-ray camera that sees inside my skull. It's on the order of a one-sided conversation and I'm doing all the talking and explaining without making a sound. But of course there's another way to look at it. Maybe it's just that I've been whiffing too much of this smoke and it's making me high. Better put a stop to that. Mustn't let that happen. Mind over matter, and so forth. You can't help breathing it in because there's nothing else to breathe. But don't let it get you. I think you can throw it off if you concentrate on the business at hand.

He said, "You ready to listen?"

Joyner nodded.

"They picked up a man," Bevan said. "They grabbed him early yesterday morning. They carted him off to a cell."

"I know that," Joyner said. He sipped smoke from the stick of weed. "I knew it when I came to see you at the hotel."

Bevan looked down at the floor. He shook his head slowly.

Then he heard Joyner laughing. It wasn't much of a sound. It was a series of very soft grunts.

He raised his head and looked at the Jamaican. He said, "Your timing was elegant. You played it satin-smooth."

"Is that a compliment?" Joyner murmured.

"Sort of."

"I like to receive compliments," Joyner said. "It puts an added flavor in the air."

"Listen, Nathan—"

"At school in England I won many prizes. I was third in my class."

"That's fine. But listen—"

"And then I come back to Jamaica with my college degree and they offer me a job as office boy. I told them—"

"Will you listen?" He said it through his teeth. "The man's name is Eustace."

"Yes, I know."

"He has a wife and children."

"You needn't tell me. I know all about Eustace."

"You know him well?"

"I've known him all my life. We were raised in the same street."

"That ought to mean something."

"In connection with what?"

"With helping him."

Joyner laughed again. This time it was louder.

"If you don't help him, he's finished," Bevan said.

The Jamaican went on laughing. The laughter was high-pitched and went higher and became a cackling noise.

"Like a hyena," Bevan said.

Joyner stopped laughing. For a moment there was nothing in his eyes.

"You're really like a hyena," Bevan said. "You feed off the dying."

The Jamaican's face glittered orange in the glow of the lamp. In his fingers the weed had burned down to a tiny stub. He raised the half-inch of weed to his tightly pursed lips and took a final drag. The smoke

stayed inside him as he let the stub drop to the floor
and carefully crushed it with his heel. Then the smoke
was coming out in tiny clouds while he said, "Let's talk
about something else. Something pleasant. Like birds
and flowers. You interested in birds and flowers?"

"Only when they're alive."

"Then let's talk about—"

"When they're dead, it's too late," Bevan said. "The
same applies to people."

"All right, we'll try music. You like music?"

"Not when it's off key."

"Would you care to hear me sing? It won't be off
key. I can sing like—"

"Like a concert artist," Bevan said. "And you can
dance with the best of them. Or do a tumbling act that
would get rave notices."

Joyner nodded very slowly. "It happens to be a fact.
I can do those things."

"Yes, I'm sure it is. It's written in smoke." He waved
his hand through the smoke haze in front of his face.
His hand felt weightless, going through the smoke. He
said, "You're really a top-flight performer. Almost the
best, but not quite. Not tonight, anyway."

"Is that wishful thinking?"

"It's more than a wish," Bevan said. "Tonight you're
coming in second."

"We'll see."

"Yes, we'll see." And then he stood up. He was
smiling at the Jamaican. He spoke very slowly and quietly. "Give it to me."

"Give you what?"

"The evidence," he said. "The broken bottle."

Joyner laughed without sound.

"Item two," Bevan said. "The blackjack."

"This is funny," Joyner said. He went on with the soundless laughter.

"Item three," Bevan said. "The number-one witness. That's you, Nathan."

"It's really funny."

"When I walk out of here, you're coming with me."

"You're quite an entertainer. Keep it up, it's very good."

"We're going to police headquarters," Bevan said.

"Tell me more," Joyner said. "More jokes."

"I said we're going to police headquarters. You're making a statement. We're giving them the bottle and the blackjack to back it up."

The laughter remained soundless but Joyner's shoulders were shaking. He was really amused. He said, "Can you actually see me doing that? It would be such a silly thing to do. They'd throw me in prison for blackmail."

"That isn't my worry," Bevan said. "My worry is Eustace."

"But why? What is Eustace to you? You don't even know the man. You've never seen him."

"That's true," Bevan said. "But I owe him something. I owe him plenty. I won't let him hang."

Joyner had stopped laughing. "You know, you're not funny now. You're a clown, but you're not funny. Perhaps the word for it is lunacy."

"Yes, it's lunacy," Bevan said. He moved slowly toward the Jamaican, who sat motionless on the edge of the cot.

"May I make a suggestion?" Joyner murmured.

"Sure." He was moving forward very slowly.

"Don't come any closer."

"Why not?"

"You'll die."

Bevan shrugged. He took another step toward the cot.

"Please don't come any closer," Joyner said. Then again his arm was a blur and the knife appeared in his hand. He held it alley-fighter style, his arm extended sideways, his fingers covering most of the blade so that what showed was less than two inches of glimmering steel.

Bevan took a sideward step, then a forward step, and another sideward step. It was more like drifting. The blade was talking to him and telling him to stay back. He replied without sound, You can scare me but you can't stop me.

And then for some vague reason he thought of Fiftieth Street and Tenth Avenue, and he heard Lita saying, Ya doing this to make up for something? Or because ya feel obligated toward the residents of low-rent neighborhoods? He answered with a smile that was aimed at the blade, his eyes saying, It isn't that, Lita. I'm sure it isn't that.

Then what is it? she persisted.

He took three steps sideward and one step forward.

He said to her, It's along the line of getting initiated. Let's call it the process of finding out the score. What I mean is…

At that moment the Jamaican was getting up from the cot and standing waiting with his legs spread and his arms out very wide and the blade making tiny circles, like the tongue of a snake. It caught the glow of the lamp and flashed bright orange against the curtain of blue-green smoke.

He went on talking to Lita. He said to her, What I mean is, there comes a time—it's a moment in the form of a dividing line between minus and plus. So you make your own choice, and if it's plus it's for real; it's getting off that fake horse on the merry-go-round going nowhere. I'm giving it a try, that's all. I'm trying to be something, so that wherever you are, you can say to yourself that it wasn't a waste of your heart and your life, that the price you paid was for a man, not a chunk of smoothly polished custom-tailored nothing.

Is that bragging? he asked himself. I don't think so. I think it's more of a realization. And somehow a pleasant thought. Yes, it's rather pleasant, and somehow I wish there were a way to get it across to a certain girl I know in Room 307 at the Laurel Rock Hotel. But of course there's no way to communicate, since all the connections are broken.

He took a forward step, then a sideward step, kept going to the side in a sort of floating dance with his body bent, his arms loose at his sides, his face showing a grin. He gave a slight shrug, a slight sigh, and lunged at the Jamaican.

Chapter Seventeen

Moonlight came down on the surface of the swimming pool, and the reflected glow floated up along the dark windows of the Laurel Rock. It shimmered silver-blue against the black ceiling in Room 307 and Cora wished it would go away. For hours she'd been trying to sleep, but every time she closed her eyes the silver-blue came through, a stream of far-off light and far-off music that gently urged her to stay awake. There's no getting rid of it, she thought. It comes from the moon and the moon is an all-night program.

And all the melodies are just one melody. It's a ballad that goes on and on, it's a river of sighs that flows without end.

Because he's gone. He finally did it. He just picked himself up and walked away.

So it's ended, I guess. But it's more than a guess. I think it's a realization. At any rate you realize there's this other man, this Atkinson. Do you want this Atkinson? You know, of course, that this Atkinson is something worthwhile. Yes, he's really something. Another thing is, he's serious about you. He's looking forward to a permanent arrangement. He's certainly the serious-permanent type and he proved it today in the garden when I behaved so absurdly, when I started to run and then fell, and whatever it was that caused it, the fact is I was completely disorganized at that moment, and if he'd wanted to he could have taken advantage of that moment, but instead of trying anything, he was strictly big brother, using his hands only to lift me up and keep me on my feet and take me away from there, take me back to the hotel. What I think is, this Atkinson wants a lifetime contract. He wants me to take off this ring I'm wearing so he can give me another. But when that happens, it'll be his privilege to...

But you don't want that. You know you don't want that.

She was out of the bed, going to the window. She stood at the window, looking down at the moonlit swimming pool. Then she gazed beyond the pool, across the garden and toward the stone wall and then the blackness beyond the wall.

It wasn't solid blackness. There were shadows and shapes, the silhouettes of sagging roofs and slanted walls. She was seeing the wooden shacks and tar-paper hovels, the slum dwellings. Here and there a lighted window showed the rutted paving of a narrow alley. She saw an overturned garbage can, or maybe it was a barrel; it was so far away she couldn't be sure. Yet somehow there was the feeling that if she wanted to, she could reach out and touch it.

Touch what? she asked herself. The garbage? the filth? You can't stand filth. You were taught long ago that filth is a crime, a downright crime. As Mother always said, "There's absolutely no excuse—"

What brings this up? Why think of Mother now? She certainly has no connection with— Well, anyway, she was constantly lecturing against getting your hands dirty. If you came in with your dress soiled she carried on something awful. Then later the anti-dirt campaign included boys, and she hired that governess named Hilda who drilled it into you that boys were dirty, you mustn't let them get near. But—what is all this? What's the connection?

She stood there at the window, staring past the stone wall that separated the Laurel Rock from the Kingston slums. Her eyes were riveted to the dark shapes of the slum dwellings and the dimly lit alleys.

That's where he is, she thought. He's out there somewhere. In all that dirt.

James, come away from there. You'll get yourself all dirty.

Then again her eyes were shut tightly and for an instant she saw the stern face of her mother. It became the stern face of the Swedish governess. Then there were the faces of the prim and stern ladies who taught at the private school and the dancing school, all these faces suddenly fading or merging to become one set of features belonging to a man. He was a big ugly man and I'm sure his name was—

But you don't remember his name. Of course you don't remember his name. But I think it was—no, please don't. Please don't try to remember. Oh, God his name was Luke. After all these years you remember his name was Luke.

He was the gardener. Mother had fired the other man when she learned he took naps in the bushes near the goldfish pond. She called the employment agency and they sent Luke. They said he was a good worker and diligent and really an excellent gardener.

I couldn't stand the sight of him. He was so big and fat and horribly ugly. His fingernails were black. I told myself not to look at him, but somehow I couldn't stop looking at him. I'd sit at the window watching him while he worked out there in the garden.

It was during Easter vacation and I was nine years old.

I was there at the window and he knew I was watching him. Every now and then he'd crinkle up that ugly face of his and smile at me. He was digging a flower bed and his hands were muddy. His fat ugly face was shiny with sweat, and once he blew his nose without using a handkerchief and it made me sick in my stomach, but I couldn't stop looking at him. "You filthy, dreadful thing," I said, but of course he couldn't hear through the window. He went on smiling at me and then he winked, and after that he beckoned with his finger, as though he were saying, Come on out here and I'll give you something.

No, I said. I'm afraid of you.

He winked again. He was leaning on the shovel. His beckoning finger moved slowly, so slowly. Come on, he said. Come out here.

It was warm in the house, but my teeth were chattering. Something lifted me up and away from the window and took me to the door and opened it for me and I went out there in the garden, where Luke was

waiting, his eyes beady like a pig's eyes, seeing the
little girl who was nine years old, who wore a pale-
green ribbon in her hair, a pale-green freshly starched
dress, and if feeling has a color, my face felt pale green
at that moment when he came close.

Cora turned away from the window. She wasn't
thinking about what she was doing while she switched
on the light and got into her clothes. It was all rapid
and mechanical, like the actions of a very efficient
worker on an assembly line. She went out of the room,
down the corridor, descended the stairway to the
lobby, and asked the desk clerk to phone for a taxi. In a
few minutes she was climbing into the taxi and saying
to the driver, "I don't know what street it's on. But it's a
house called Winnie's Place."

"Barry Street," the driver said. Then he turned and
looked at her. "You sure about dis? You sure you want
to go dere?"

Her hand moved automatically, the gesture telling
him to get started.

The taxi moved slowly. Cora opened her purse and
took out a five-dollar bill. She leaned forward and
showed the money to the driver. "If you hurry it up,"
she said, "you'll benefit. I won't ask for change."

The driver's foot pressed hard on the gas pedal. The
taxi screeched around a corner. Cora sat rigidly on the
edge of the seat, her hands folded tightly in her lap.
The driver was saying something but she didn't hear.
Her eyes were blank and not focused on anything. The
sound that came from her was the clicking sound of

her chattering teeth. The driver was asking if she had a chill; he couldn't understand why she was shivering. He kept asking her about it but she didn't hear.

"You go in alone?" the driver asked. He was pulling up on the brake and reaching back to open the door for her. As she climbed out of the taxi she handed him the five-dollar bill and he said, "Perhaps if you require some aid—"

"No," she said. She had turned and was facing the one-story wooden house. She saw that the windows were lighted.

"You wish me to wait?" the driver asked.

"All right," she said. She moved quickly to the doorstep and knocked on the door. She hit it hard with her fist and kept hitting it until it opened. She saw the face of the Jamaican woman who stood there looking her up and down. Then the woman stepped back, allowing her to enter.

She went in. The woman closed the door. Cora said, "I'm looking for—"

"I know," Winnie said. "De white mon. De American tourist."

"Yes. He drinks a lot and—"

"He not drinking now," Winnie said.

Something has happened, Cora thought. But the thought didn't show on her face. Nothing showed on her face. She spoke quietly. "Tell me where he is."

Winnie didn't say anything.

"Please tell me," Cora said. "I'm his wife."

"His wife?" Winnie's head was slanted. Her eyes were narrowed with doubt. "He not say to me he has wife."

"I'm saying it. Don't you believe me?"

"Not yet," Winnie said. "Dere is contradiction here. He not seem like mon who has wife. He seem very lonely, like someone not wanted."

Cora winced slightly. For a moment her shoulders slumped. Then again she stood straight and rigid, and her voice was thin and tight as she said, "If you know where he is, you'll tell me. You can't keep me from—"

"Yes, I can," Winnie said. "I not let you interfere. Dis issue not include you, lady. It very important issue and I not allow you to spoil it."

"Spoil what? What are you talking about?"

"He performing an errand," Winnie said. "Dat why you find my house lit up. I have been sitting here waiting—hoping he come out of it alive."

Cora moved mechanically. She was clutching the wrists of the woman. "Then he needs me," she said. "Wherever he is, he needs me."

"Let go, please. You hurt my wrists."

"He needs me!"

"What tells you dat? How you know for sure?"

"I just know it. I feel it."

It was quiet and their eyes were riveted together. The quiet was like a wire stretching and vibrating.

Then it broke. Winnie said, "You care for de mon, you must go to de mon." She looked down at the hands that held her wrists. The hands fell away. She walked to the door and opened it and said, "Morgan's Alley. De house number is seventeen."

Cora nodded. She murmured aloud to herself, "Seventeen."

"Morgan's Alley. Say it so you will remember."

"Seventeen Morgan's Alley," Cora said. She hurried through the doorway and across the rutted paving and climbed into the waiting taxi.

Winnie stood in the doorway watching the taxi as it moved away and gained speed. The taillights became small and then smaller and finally vanished in the darkness. Winnie turned and went into the house. She seated herself in a splintered chair near the splintered, sagging bar. For several minutes she sat there looking at the floor. Then all at once she stiffened. She stood up and moved toward the door and opened it and walked out of the house.

Chapter Eighteen

At the intersection of Barry Street and Morgan's Alley the taxi came to a stop and the driver said, "You get out here."

"How far do I walk?"

"Not far." He gestured with his thumb. "Down dat way."

"Why can't you drive me there?"

"De alley not wide enough."

"Sure it is. You can make it."

"Not wide enough," the driver said "Besides, de path it bumpy. Too many holes. We maybe get stuck."

"The holes aren't that deep."

"Lady, I take you dis far and no furder. You please get out here."

"What's the matter?" Cora asked.

He didn't answer. He leaned across the seat and reached toward the rear door and opened it for her, motioning for her to get out.

She didn't move. She said, "What's the matter with you? Are you afraid?"

The driver sat there waiting for her to get out of the taxi.

"I think you're afraid," she said. And then, as he turned and looked at her, "That's silly, of course. There's nothing to be afraid of."

"Den why your face so pale? Why your teeth make noise like little motorboat?"

"Is that what it sounds like?" She heard it then. It seemed to come from very far away, yet she knew it came from her own mouth. I ought to stop that, she thought, and she said aloud, "I really ought to stop it."

The driver squirmed. His eyes were wide. Now he stared past her, at the darkness and stillness of the alley. His face showed that he was very anxious to get away from here.

Cora climbed out of the taxi. She was opening her purse and saying, "What do I owe you?"

"You pay me already," the driver said. He was pulling at the handle of the rear door, slamming it shut. For an instant his eyes were hungry, aiming at the opened purse. But his brain was focused on the need to get away and get away fast. He shoved the gear shift, his foot hit the gas pedal, and the taxi shot across the intersection and went speeding away down Barry Street.

Cora turned and faced the alley, which seemed more like a tunnel. Seventeen, she said to herself. Seventeen Morgan's Alley. She started to walk, moving along a diagonal that took her toward a moonlit doorway that showed a chalked number. The number was carelessly scrawled and somewhat erased by time and weather and she couldn't make it out. She came closer and saw it was 37. The adjoining doorway was not numbered. She was moving slowly through the alley, staying close to the doorways and looking for chalked numbers and seeing none and going back to find 37 again so she could start counting the houses.

Not really houses, she thought. More on the order of enlarged rat traps. Falling apart. And the air, the smell. The smell is awful. How can they stand it? How can they live here? It's ghastly, it's really ghastly to know that people actually live here. Look at that cat. Oh no, don't come near me, please go away. Oh, thank God it's walking away. But look at it, just look at it. Maybe it's half rat or half dog. But that's impossible, of course. Or maybe not. Maybe anything is possible in this place. If only you could walk with your eyes closed so you wouldn't see. Especially the dirt. All this dirt. It seems to come in a stream through the doorways and flow like syrupy scum into your pores, your eyes, and your mouth. I can't take this. I feel like throwing up. There's that cat again and it has something in its mouth. It's a mouse. It's a big mouse. No, it's a rat, and look at all that blood. Oh, Mother, come and get me, take me away from here! But this door is 33 and this one here is 31 and this one must be 29 and—

She came to a stop. Her hand came up to her mouth. She pressed her hand very hard against her stomach. Something tugged at her eyes and it seemed to her that her eyes were coming out of her face.

Moving toward her very slowly from the doorway of 29, the big Australian seaman was squinting, his head tilted forward and slightly slanted as he tried to get her in focus. At first he'd thought the moonlight was playing tricks and changing the color of the skin of the woman he had been waiting for. Then, as he came closer, he thought, This one's really white. And smaller than the other one. Much skinnier. Much prettier, too. Like a delicate flower, soft and milky-white, and under that dress she's…

Cora managed to close her eyes. She opened them and he was there. She closed them and opened them and he was there. She stood rigidly, staring at him, seeing the bloated face, the bloated belly, the heavy thighs that strained against the grimy white duck trousers. His huge hands were flat against his sides, the fingers spread wide, and she looked at the hairy hands and the black fingernails.

Hainesworth grinned at her. His teeth showed yellow. His thick lips were wet and flapping slowly as he mumbled something she didn't hear.

It's Luke, she thought. It's Luke, the gardener. And somehow there was no such thing as time and it wasn't Morgan's Alley. It was the lawn outside the house and she was wearing a pale-green ribbon in her hair, and the pale-green dress freshly starched. It was during Easter vacation and she was nine years old.

Again he said something that she couldn't hear. He went on talking and she made some reply but she had no idea what it was.

Hainesworth came closer. He was breathing heavily. He moved in quickly and reached for her and grabbed her, but she wriggled away. Then she turned and started to run and stumbled, going to her knees. Hainesworth came in again and took her wrist and pulled her arm behind her back. With his other hand he covered her mouth. She twisted her head convulsively and his middle finger went between her teeth. Before he could pull it out she was biting, and he let out a groan and she bit harder. Her teeth cut through the thick flesh of his finger and she was tasting his blood.

Spit it out, she thought. It's nasty stuff, it's dirty. Please spit it out. She opened her mouth to spit it out, gagging with her head lowered and trying to get it out, but still tasting the blood flavor, the dirt flavor.

Hainesworth looked at his bleeding finger, seeing the teeth marks. But he wasn't groaning now, and he didn't feel the deep cuts. He said, "So you bite, do you? Well that's the way I like it, my gal."

She was up on her feet, trying again to get away, but Hainesworth was faster and he wrapped his arms around her middle and squeezed. The breath rushed out of her mouth and she tried to inhale but it felt as though her lungs were crushed. She reached back, her fingers jabbing, her fingernails finding the flesh of his face. He squeezed harder, lifting her off the ground. He's breaking me in half, she thought, and in a tiny channel of her mind she felt self-pity. But the other channels were all animal and the primary directive was to her arms and hands and fingernails. Her fingernails were hooks going in deep, coming out and going in again. The blood from his clawed face flowed over her fingers. She reached higher along his face, trying to find his eyes.

Her thumbnail caught him just under the eye. He threw his head back as the blood spurted from the open pocket. He squeezed very hard and she made a gurgling noise. Her arms came down limp and her head drooped. Then her knees gave way as he released the grip around her middle.

"Hey. You fainted?" he asked.

She answered with a hissing sound.

"That's fine," he said. "That's just fine."

His big hand came down on her head. He had a handful of her hair and he pulled hard. Again she made the hissing sound, and as he lifted her by her hair she swung her leg, then both legs, one-two, one-two. Her sharp-pointed shoes banged against his shins. He came in very close and reached down and caught her behind her knees, then picked her up and held her horizontal, the way they hold the wriggling salmon. She went on kicking, trying to get him again with her fingernails and her teeth. Her fingernails found his neck and her teeth took the flesh of his lower jaw while he carried her across the alley and through the narrow space between the shacks.

It was a very narrow space and he had difficulty getting through. He had to move sideways with the wriggling, kicking burden. His grin widened as the narrow space between the shacks was suddenly a larger space, and he said to her, "We've arrived."

He had her close to the wall in the back yard of 29. The soil was soft and lumpy. There were some tin cans and chunks of broken crockery and other rubbish scattered about, and in that immediate area he kicked the litter aside. When the space was reasonably cleared, he lifted her higher, then flung her to the ground.

She came down hard on her side but didn't feel the

impact. In the instant that she hit the ground she was trying to get up. She couldn't make it. The effort caused her to roll over, face down. Then something kept her there, and as she attempted to lift her head she felt the pressure that was just too heavy, too much. It was his heavy hands pushing down on her spine and her head, forcing her face into the dirt.

The dirt was in her eyes and nose and mouth. She was trying to breathe and more dirt came in. She couldn't spit it out; she was eating it. Some of it actually went down, and she thought, That does it. Now you'll pass out. But she didn't pass out. It had the opposite effect, as though she'd taken a stimulant. And as more dirt came into her mouth she thought, It's something stronger than any pharmacy can offer. Because you're tasting earth and there's nothing so real as the earth, nothing truer. So it isn't dirt, it's a cleanser. Or you might call it an eraser. It rubs out all the blurred images of a mother and a governess and all the strict teachers in private school and dancing school. They're making an exit now, they're really making a rapid exit.

Yes, they're going away like a committee that's been voted down after years and years of fouling up procedure. Because they blocked every move to clarify the issue. I mean the issue of growing up to be a woman instead of a meaningless ornament wearing a dress.

Yes, because they drilled it into you that you were sugar and spice and everything nice, while on the other hand the masculine gender is rats and snails and puppy dogs' tails, and so forth and so forth. And then when you're nine years old, just getting old enough to wonder if they're stretching the point, along comes the gardener.

Along comes Luke with his dirty face and dirty hands to make that drilled-in theory a nailed-down, sealed-in fact. He took you in the bushes near the goldfish pond and lifted your dress and you said, "What are you doing?" and he said, "It won't hurt," and then you wondered what was happening while it happened. It really wasn't much. You didn't faint or go into convulsions, you didn't even bleed. All he did was—

You never told Mother or Hilda or anyone at all. The next day Luke went away and didn't come back. But the eyes of Luke never went away. The filthy eyes of Luke were inside you, always looking at something very deep inside you and coming closer and closer. His burning filthy eyes became the eyes of anything masculine that looks at something female and comes closer.

So that later in the years of the nights in the bed with James...But in the darkness of the room you couldn't see his face, so it was never James, it was always the gardener.

And there it is. Now you know. You were constantly pulling away from what you thought was something dirty, messy, horrible, when all the time it was clean and pure, because he's your mate and he adores you. I think the proof of that is evident. Yes, I'm inclined to say it's quite evident. It's based on the fact that he's stayed with you all these years. So from one point of view he's the buffoon who puts up with the frigid wife, the weak-kneed, weak-brained clown who guzzles much too much alcohol and becomes a nonentity labeled "Incapable." From a clearer point of view, he's more of a man than most men. He's on the Galahad side. Oh, yes, he's right up there with all the Galahads who walk that lonely road of endless sacrifice. So now you know, girl. Now you know what needs to be done, what you want to do, what you're aching to do from here on in. But is it too late for that?

Just then the earth became a wall that slanted away from her face. The seaman was rolling her over so that she was flat on her back. He had one hand pushing down hard on her shoulder, his other hand lifting her skirt. She looked at his eyes and saw the eyes of the gardener coming closer, and she reached out to the side and groped through lumpy soil and weeds and pebbles. Her eyes were tightly shut and she went on groping then she felt the jagged hardness of something half buried in the ground. She could feel it was a large stone and she tugged at it, clawing and twisting and wrenching to pull it free. He was on her now and starting to do something, but she was very far away from that. The only feeling she had was of the large chunk of jagged stone coming into her hand. The weight of it was almost too much for her arm, yet somehow her arm moved quickly, the stone bashing against the side of his head, hitting him there again and again and then again.

The seaman fell away from her. He was in a half-sitting position, resting back on his elbow. His mouth was wide open and it was as though he wanted to say something. He remained in that position while the blood came gushing from his mouth and nose, something yellow-gray seeping from his ears and something else that was wet-gray oozing from the side of his head. Then his elbows gave way, and he was reclining on his back, his mouth staying open and still trying to say something while he died.

Cora lifted herself to her feet. For a few moment she stood looking at the corpse. As she turned away from it she was giggling.

She didn't know she was giggling. She didn't know she was moving through the narrow space between the shacks and coming out on Morgan's Alley. She went on giggling as she walked very slowly along a zig-zag route that seemed to be taking her nowhere, but was actually taking her toward Number 17.

Her eyes were focused on the doorways. But she couldn't count the doorways because on each door there was a face and it was the face of the corpse with its head bashed and the wet-gray oozing out. She wished the face would go away, but it stayed, and she went on giggling.

It was the only sound she heard. She didn't hear the noise of the police car coming down the alley. The car was coming fast, coming from behind with its horn sustaining a high-pitched blast, telling her to get out of the way. She hopped aside automatically, instinctively. She didn't see the police car flashing past, didn't see it coming to a sudden stop down there in the darkness not very far away. The only thing she saw was the face of the corpse, which caused her to giggle. But her legs were moving again and it was as though something were pushing her toward Number 17.

The police car was parked beside Number 17. Some policemen emerged, and then a small man with yellow-gray skin and slanted eyes, followed by a black woman. One of the policemen opened the door of Number 17, then stood aside, and the small man with slanted eyes walked in. He was wearing a bathrobe and bedroom slippers. The others filed in behind him.

As Cora approached the opened door a voice from somewhere told her that this was Number 17 and she entered giggling. A moment later she saw the face of the wounded man who was flat on his back on the floor. She walked toward the wounded man, whose face obliterated forever the face of the slain Luke. She stopped giggling. But then her legs gave way, and as she sagged toward the floor, they grabbed her.

Chapter Nineteen

Like oranges falling out of a tree, Bevan thought. What he saw were spheres of orange light that danced against a dark-gray curtain. He passed out again and when he came to he heard voices, but he had no idea what they were saying. Then again he drifted out of it and stayed out for what seemed hours, but it was only a matter of minutes. Now someone was helping him to sit up and someone else was trying to give him a drink of water. He blinked several times and saw the shiny white helmets and dark faces and white jackets of the policemen. One of them was using a pair of scissors to cut some adhesive tape. He saw a small dark-green metal box with a small square of white painted on the side, in the center of the white square a little cross painted red, signifying that this was a first-aid kit, and he thought, Someone's been hurt.

Then he felt the pressure of the bandages. He was wearing several bandages. There was one wrapped thickly around his right arm from the elbow all the way up to the shoulder. Another bandage circled his left shoulder, and still another was bound around his middle, and there were more on both legs just above the knees. But under the pressure you don't feel anything, he thought. They must have given you a needle, or something. When it wears off you'll catch hell from these cuts. You're sure cut up very nicely. He did some fancy carving with that blade. I guess that's what knocked you out, losing all that blood. Or maybe you just ran out of gas and hit the floor. So that makes you the loser, the fumbler. You let him get away.

But now his eyes were able to focus and he gazed across the room and saw them in the dim orange glow of the lamp near the cot. There were two of them sitting on the edge of the cot.

One of them was Nathan, whose face was bruised. Nathan had a purplish lump over his left eye. His mouth was puffed and bleeding, and the right side of his jaw was extremely swollen. The other man was Inspector Archinroy in a bathrobe. He was writing something in a notebook while Nathan talked quietly through the puffed and bleeding lips. On the Inspector's lap there was a blackjack, and on the cot at the Inspector's side there was a broken bottle.

For some moments Bevan focused on the broken bottle. Then he turned his head just a little and saw Winnie, who stood near the cot with her arms folded. She was listening intently to what Nathan was saying. She was nodding slowly.

At Bevan's shoulder a voice said, "It needs more bandage. Here, along his ribs."

"There is no more bandage. We use it all up." This was a policeman's voice.

The other voice said, "Give me the scissors."

"To cut your dress? But that might infect the wound. Your dress is all dirty."

"Then I'll use what I have underneath. Give me the scissors."

"But you are wearing only— Look, lady, the ambulance will be here soon."

"Please give me the scissors." Then a pause, and then, "Thank you," and after that he heard the sound of the scissors snipping fabric. He couldn't turn his head to look at her because now they'd eased him over on his side. He felt her hands on his bare flesh as she applied the improvised bandage to his ribs, up near the armpit. The touch of her hands was warm and soft. Feels nice, he thought. Feels so nice.